The Nun

Sandra Shwayder Sanchez

Plain View Press
http://plainviewpress.net

3800 N. Lamar, Suite 730-260
Austin, TX 78756

ISBN: 978-0-911051-60-5
Library of Congress Control Number: 91-066436

Cover art photo by Sandra Shwayder Sanchez
Cover design by Pam Knight

Acknowledgements

I owe thanks to many people who nurtured the literary muse in my life: to my mother Jeanne for surrounding my childhood with literature, music and art, to my father Bud for reading to me at a very early age and setting an example of integrity with his word, to my stepmother Carol whose quiet strength and vigilant love kept him among us longer than I could otherwise have hoped, to my friend and role model of half a century Ita Willen who started me writing stories, to my old friend Ugo Scotto who's enthusiasm kept me writing and to Jack Salamanca who's praise gave me confidence, to Susan Bright and Peter Burnham who not only published early work but who's editorial feedback and example of social responsibility in literature was better than an MFA program for me, to Pam Knight who has so courageously and conscientiously kept Susan's legacy alive, to my husband Ed Sanchez who for twenty years has graciously shared me with so many fictional characters and to my daughters Rachel and Sara who learned a little from me but taught me so much more.

"Life is journey and death a destination"

This book is dedicated to those who have arrived: Sol and Ida Shwayder, Bernard and Lillian Hershorn, Bud Shwayder, Jeanne H. Segal, brother Dougie who's journey was short but left the world an infinitely better place, and last but not least to Susan Bright, poet, publisher, activist and a light unto all.

Contents

Part 1

Chapter I

Each woman had, besides the communal tasks of chanting and prayer, a practical task to accomplish. One supervised the young girls who came from outside to work in the weaving room. In exchange for their labor, they learned a trade and learned it well. Another of the nuns oversaw other girls in the laundry work and when she saw them well into their task, she went to help in the garden. All the nuns worked in the garden. Their sustenance depended on it and they could get no one else to come to help with this vital work. Of all the nuns, Odyssia was the one who spent most time in the garden, daily in fact, whatever the weather, and she had no other task. All spring and summer she worked a long hard day, but in the fall, when the harvest had been dried, hung, pickled and stored, Sia found herself with entire afternoons free to spend in the woods exploring.

During one of her walks in the woods when the forest seemed woven of contrasting and mellowing greens and reds, she met Magi. She was curious when she first met Magi whether she was a man or a woman, and she never really could be sure, but she preferred to think that Magi was female and Magi herself didn't seem to care. She was very square, too solid to be considered fat, with the beginnings of breasts and very strong mannish arms and hands. She had the slightest mustache and was most extraordinarily hairy all over her body and face. Her facial features were badly molded, thick and roughed in and her skin was bumpy and pitted. She dressed in filthy men's clothing and large boots.

The first time Sia saw her in the woods she was frightened and hid in a ravine formed by a dried up stream. As she watched from her hiding place in the leaves she saw Magi choose a newly felled log. She stripped off the bark and caressed the wood, touching and examining it and this intrigued Sia. Later Sia followed Magi through the woods to a small hut built of logs filled in with mud and roofed with long grasses dried in the sun. Nearby was another log hut, three sided with a roof and filled with beautifully carved wooden figures.

The figures were all that Magi was not, tall and thin with flowing drapery revealing only slightly the full feminine shapes of hips and breasts beneath.

The faces were thin with long sharp noses and large eyes under exquisitely sculpted lids. Oddly enough the lips were not well done. But the hands were the best of all, long thin-fingered hands delicately holding goblets or flowers or the folds of a robe. These sculptures were Magi's rebellion against the inescapable ugliness of herself, her challenge to God. Sia herself was as beautiful as the statues, but it had not brought her joy, inviting only envy and lust, and she sought to hide in the cloisters.

Every day that fall, Sia had followed Magi through the woods and when Magi was away from the hut she went herself to get a closer look at the statues. She examined them carefully as she listened for Magi's approach and she was also careful to note the light in order to know the time and be back in time for the evening meal and prayers. Often she wondered if she shouldn't wait for Magi and speak to her (him? she hadn't yet decided) and ask if she could learn to carve figures herself. She always ended up by deciding against it because Magi's appearance frightened her. But it was meant that she should learn this art and one afternoon in late November Magi surprised her among the statues. Sia stood quietly waiting for Magi's reaction and carefully concealing her own fear. Magi was kind from the start and Sia never told her about her fear, not wishing to hurt her feelings.

Magi never talked much; the shortest conversation seemed to make her hoarse and over excited. She had lived alone in the woods for many years with only the trees for company.

Now Sia began to spend all her afternoons carving the blocks of wood Magi allotted her. Magi rarely spoke but silently guided her pupil and communicated a great love and pride in Sia's work, for these carvings were her children and grandchildren. Sia was working now on a hand, a very rough old hand, long fingered, and shaped like her own left hand which she occasionally held up as a model, staring at the beauty of her own left hand as if it were totally detached from her person, a hand. She imagined her own hand with flesh of pine, grained and whorled and ageless. Often Sia saw the older nuns, moving stiffly, and angular, change into dark wood and later she would carve them. She worked slowly and patiently, feeling that she had forever to learn and confident that she would learn all she needed to create the most perfect statues in wood and later (as Magi promised) in stone.

At first she worked only with pine because it was soft and easy to carve, but often she would accidentally break or tear the wood and ruin an otherwise perfect carving. At first she carved only the pieces Magi brought to her. But soon she decided she must learn to choose her own wood and to carve in different kinds of wood. She learned to identify the different kinds of trees by their bark instead of merely their leaves and she learned what the different woods were like, the malleability, the quality of the grain and how their own secret patterns complimented the figures she would carve in them. She learned to look for trees that had died from drought or had frozen in an unusually harsh winter, trees that died perfect, not maimed by disease or rot, their limbs still reaching and graceful, the bark slowly dropping off as the dead wood inside dried and shrank inward. Such wood could be used almost as soon as it was cut. But they also cut living trees, (the forest was generous) and these, dripping with sap, their translucent tree blood, were set upright in the drying shed where they would stand for years before being carved. These trees had been alive, still showed the signs of life, took years to completely lose their livingness—and Sia felt rapport with them. Walking in the woods, she felt as though she floated among the bones of her own body.

There were other uses for the wood besides artistic. To build another small, three-sided shed they cut tall, straight and thin pine poles. Every chore was a pleasure to Sia. Magi set her to stripping the bark from these poles. The bark came off easily in long fragrant strips that curled and enticed her. While still supple these strips of bark were woven by Sia into mats and baskets to serve a variety of purposes. The wood beneath was golden and succulent and would only need to age a short time before it could be used for building. Every day Sia checked the poles, looking at them as if to see through the outermost layer of sap bark to the whorls that told the trees story, every year a different succession of rain and sun, every inch a different pattern in the grain. Cutting across the grain, even that immeasurable width separated into two distinct patterns, similar but never the same. What should have been two mirror images were instead two different universes separated by a kind of time that could not be counted or conceived.

Sia learned to carve walnut that, despite its hardness, yielded easily to her tools. But more than walnut, she liked to carve in open-grained woods that guided, the polished concentricities of line giving a voluptuous quality to a cheek, an arm, the fold of a robe. And all the while Sia mused over the infinity of design as if trying to decipher the writing of an ancient, extinct race, as if these trees, these dead trees, were the self-mummified artifacts of another world.

She began to feel the slight disturbances of half recognized memories and yearned to relive a past that spanned a thousand years in all directions, and then she would immerse herself for hours in the constantly changing shapes of water. She imagined the stones beneath being carved before her eyes as if each moment were a hundred years and she herself eternal in seeing. It was a thought she had in vision rather than words. And she would watch, as well, the leaves blowing lightly in the breeze created by the fast-moving stream, the leaves and the branches that carved the air around them into shapes, and she held these shapes of air in her eyes. She did not like touching things separately with her fingers, it made her feel so outside. She wished she could be absorbed into the forest and feel a part of it. Her thoughts were strange and unspeakable wishing to be the streambed, She could not mention these desires to anyone. They had the sound of carnality, even worse, a strange and unique sort of carnality.

She was not afraid of these thoughts as she was of visions of men, but she knew better than to share them. With the other nuns, she talked about the weather and the garden. Sometimes events from uneventful childhoods were recalled, little stories with little points. She talked with half of her mind while the other half watched their faces, their hands, analyzed their accents, some from towns, some from the countryside, some richer, some poorer. She could tell where a woman was from by her choice of words, the way she ordered the words, the way she drew out or cut short certain vowels; Sia would always find the pattern in their speech, the shape of it.

Then she stopped talking and resented it when the nuns at the cloister made small talk around her or to her and interrupted her pondering, as if their chatter somehow cut her off from her from her introspective destination. She felt that she understood Magi and between them speech was not necessary and that among those who did not understand her; speech was not useful. The singing, that abstract flowing of human sound, soothed her and made vivid the visions she sought. She grew to love the singing, to crave it, and she kept it always in her mind as a kind of guide to the innermost whorls of her own history, her soul's as yet unlived memories. But even this modulated sound of the living present she could only tolerate either at a distance, very far and faint, or very close, vibrating in her head, either extreme of distance acoustically distorting and dehumanizing the music, moving it from exterior reality to interior vision. And thus everything she touched, heard, smelled, saw she internalized, absorbed into her dream, made ancient and distant, all her senses working to illuminate that memory lost in such a deep place in her soul.

If anyone noticed her growing introspective preoccupation, they would naturally attribute it to a strong religious vocation and no one tried seriously to intrude upon her waking dream. Moving as she did through myriad simultaneous incarnations, the ordinary time of the convent passed unnoticed, winter, spring, summer, fall, she couldn't quite tell how many of them, and often she simply telescoped all the summers into one, all the winters into one. It might have been two years that passed as she carved instead of ten. But then she'd take a log that she had cut fresh and living from the forest and it was ready now for the tools and she'd know that she was growing older. She could carve as well as Magi in wood but she never questioned Magi about her promise to teach her to carve in stone, the promise had been made and she trusted that it would be fulfilled when the time was right. In preparation for that time she began to handle stone, to work with it. She built a small hut of stone, fitting the pieces so the walls were strong without mortar. To Sia each stone was unique and she chose them carefully. At first the stones seemed heavy but she grew stronger and surprised herself with what she could lift and carry. Sometimes she came to a problem with her carving, some indecision, a feeling that she was no longer following the wood, not really seeing it properly and then she would pick and pile her stones, a kind of active meditation, until she could return to the wood and finish her task. It was in this way that the hut was built. Magi never mentioned it.

Magi worked alone now, no longer guiding Sia as she also worked alone, each alone with wood. But Sia found she learned more and more, by doing, and sometimes by watching Magi, quietly and from a proper distance. Her figures were beautiful, as beautiful as any she had ever seen anywhere, and they grew out of her, out of a skill she was hardly even aware of, her hands seeming to have souls of their own. But it was the soul of the wood that guided the sculpture; it was always there in the grain—the lines she would follow, the design.

When each figure was finished she loved it, and she never thought about what would become of it. There were many statues lined up in the sheds, but occasionally Magi took one to a nearby village. She got a ride in a cart with a man who came by regularly though infrequently and there she traded a statue for cloth and grains, wine and oil. That is the way it seemed to Sia.

Actually Magi sold the figures to a man from a large city who came to the village to meet her and to buy other things in the village and then Magi could buy whatever she needed, which wasn't much. Magi probably knew what would become of the figures but Sia never asked so Magi never told her. Magi would make a new pair of trousers with the cloth she bought and with the old ones she would make a sack to hold chips of bark for the fire.

It interested Sia that Magi grew nothing of her own but lived entirely from the forest. She gathered herbs that grew wild all around, some to drink, some to rub on the skin for various ailments, some to tie up in bunches and hang from the ceiling for some pagan token. She set traps of her own clever and complicated design to catch small animals to eat and used the herbs to flavor the water she boiled the wild meat in. Sometimes she caught fish in the streams but she complained that it took too long. Mostly she wanted the fish oil which she boiled with wine and beeswax from abandoned hives to make a substance she rubbed on the finished statues to protect them. Although it was common practice, Magi did not paint her wood statues. She burned rotten wood she found lying on the ground and bark and wood chips and she carved the figures that when sold for money enabled her to buy whatever the forest had failed to provide. Her life was very simple, poor perhaps in the eyes of some, but she had surrounded herself with a wealth of beauty few could afford.

Sia never shared a meal with Magi for she would always go from the woods to the convent for the prayers and meals she shared only half consciously with a dozen other nuns. And Magi never invited her. Nor did Sia ever question Magi about her routine for survival. But she watched intently everything that Magi did and noticed every object in her home. Like working with the stones, these observations seemed suitable preparation for some part of her future.

Chapter II

Sia hungered for the wood and felt nourished by it even while, in fact, she grew thinner with actual hunger. The fall harvest had not been good and late frosts the spring before had blighted the blossoms on the fruit trees so that now there were no fruits to dry and store of food each year were rationed accordingly. This year no one ever felt fully satisfied, but no one starved. It was not so among the neighboring countrymen and women.

Although everyone started out with the same understanding of the facts of their existence, their dependence on the weather and the whims of the gods (oh yes they worshipped God, but always there was an undercurrent of paganism, of wheedling and appeasing and raillery against the myriad gods of unpredictable chance, of frosts or hail, drought or molding damp, of insects and animals and even human forgetfulness and laziness and exhaustion and despair), although everyone began the season with the same understanding of what lay ahead, they all used this knowledge differently. Not many could control the effects of their personalities on their reason. Understanding this, the abbess did not judge as stupid or lazy or extravagant the repeated poor planning of her neighbors, nor did she know that they judged her as arrogant. But in accepting as normal their extremes, reaping extravagant joy one day, a joy usually measured in wine and food and giving violent expression to their suffering and poverty the next, she saw no need or perhaps no hope, in trying to change them, to even out the chasms between want and plenty. She accepted them, ignored them and let nature take its course.

Meantime the nuns in their convent, like well-organized ants, weathered the seasons with little variation from year to year, mostly unaware of the violent ups and down of their neighbors. And as Sia became more and more and more aloof from the convent community itself, she became even less aware of the "outside world", not even listening to bits of gossip that rippled through the kitchen and workrooms. The relationship of the nuns to the world around them was largely a matter of rumor and innuendo, never really clear to anyone, but each woman had her own perception subtly different from all the other and responded with her own personal reaction of fear or contempt or relief. Sia alone had ceased entirely to think about it. She was totally surrounded by images of perfect beauty unmarred by the incongruities of human personality. She felt herself grained and old and immune as ok.

All around them resentment festered, poisoning the air, perversely nourished by the famine and the deaths of children. The nuns, sensing it, could not accurately gauge it. Sia was completely unaware of it.

In the evenings, walking back to prayers, Sia measured the distance yet to go by the chants of the nuns, their voices drifting like mist through the trees to her and only becoming real when she entered the chambers of stone. She was so accustomed to this sound she often heard it at other times and places, deeper in the woods where she couldn't possibly hear them, and yet she did hear them, her memory twisting the random sounds of birds and crickets and streams into the orderly plainsong of nuns singing through stone.

This evening the singing sound reached her earlier and she thought nothing of it, but as she came within sight of the convent, she became uneasily aware of discordant sounds, and then abruptly she heard it quite clearly, a scream, Sia stopped to listen carefully and let this confusion of sound and then, yes, it was screaming: the screaming of women in terror and pain and mingled with this, men laughing. The men were extravagant, reaping their harvest of despair. They had taken the food stored up by the nuns for their wives and children, and now they were taking the women, raping and killing them and laughing because now they were all equal, grieving and screaming and hurt, by God.

It took a long time and the vengeful energy of two or three men with dead and starving children. Already some of the men were worried that they all would be punished for their sin, but others had learned that all was chance and their god was indifferent, malicious and life was his joke. They hadn't reasoned it out in their minds; they knew it in their brutal souls. But regardless of God, regardless of sin and punishment, regardless of the vicissitudes of pure chance, there it was: a courtyard full of a dozen dead and dying women. Anyone who still whimpered was quickly put out of her misery and the women were pyred in the courtyard atop their own heavy furnishings and tapestries.

After the convulsions of slaughter came the calm of necessity. This one time the countrymen were well-organized, while some stayed to cremate the bodies, others packed up their booty of dried peas and flour, oil and wine, and carefully conveyed them to their families, this one time distributing everything equally among their numbers and rationing it all out to last the winter.

It had been a small convent, remote and isolated. The larger world plagued with wars and heresies and more far-reaching resentments paid no attention to its end.

Sia herself was initially unaffected by what had happened. Like a terrible nightmare it traumatized her while she watched, but once over it's implications gave way to more mundane anxieties. For two or three days she was totally concerned with fear for herself and hid in the woods, hungry, damp and freezing but hardly daring to move. She listened to the crackle of burning timbers and the crash of unsupported stones trying to detect behind these noises the sounds of men. But the men were gone. Then she began to move cautiously back through the woods to Magi's hut.

It was an agonizing slow walk, straining for silence, stopping to listen, mistrustful of the silence and afraid of every sound. It took her an entire day to get to Magi's and then she found Magi dead also. She'd been dead for a couple of days now and there was an odor despite the cold. Sia broke four days of utter, strained silence and screamed and screamed in terror, thinking that Magi had been another victim of the peasants. But why? She had nothing they could want or envy. Superstition perhaps? It happened, Sia knew. But Magi's body, When Sia looked closer, trembling and desperate, was not mutilated and her expression was not stricken or afraid Sia prayed to know how Magi died but God told her nothing.

Sia told herself that she was truly forsaken. She calmed down because she had no choice; there was no one else to answer her need. And she thought about what had to be done. Magi's body had to be buried, and lacking strength to carry it, Sia used patience and ingenuity to lever and roll the heavy body into a shallow ravine. First she covered the body with leaves, the matted damp leaves of the forest floor, and with large thick pieces of moss that she peeled off boulders in the stream and with bark she peeled from trees. There was nowhere she could dig soil for the grave, the thinnest layer of soil over rock. she took rushes meant for roofing and then she began to gather stones. She was all night carrying stones to cover the grave, her eyes became accustomed to the dark and she thought constantly of vultures and wild dogs. Sia carried the stones until morning when she could see that it was enough.

Her labor warmed her and the terror of the last few days left her unable to eat. For awhile she could concentrate only on her need to think out her survival. She had to reorganize her life, starting with nothing. She had no sense of direction and would not have dared seek out other people for help. She remembered Magi's traps and herbs but she was suddenly aware of her exhaustion and put off an inventory until after she'd slept. She rolled herself up in Magi's sooty blanket and slept from shortly after sunrise to shortly before sunrise of the next day. She kept dreaming of waking and seeing people, the men, the murderers, talking rationally to her as if nothing had happened and herself trying to get up, trying to talk back to them, but unable to, feeling too tired, feeling pulled down by the heavy tiredness in her body and for a long time after she really did wake up she thought they had been there. It was hours before she realized she had been asleep the whole time

She felt weak and dizzy and realized she must eat something soon. The traps would have been in a certain place in the hut if they were in the hut but she did not find them so she went out to look for them, walking where she had seen Magi walk. Two were empty but in the third an animal had bled or starved to death. The stench and the buzzing of flies frightened and disgusted her and she did not go near it. She examined the other traps to see how they were set, sprang one and reset it. She checked the traps twice daily as Magi had done and killed whatever small animals she found struggling in them with a blow on the head.

Magi had been quick and sure and the animals died quickly, stunned painlessly into death. Sia's first attempts were clumsy and, overcome with guilt and panic, she smashed and maimed squealing rabbits and squirrels which were then not fit to eat and she dreamed their slow agonizing and bewildered suffering nightly. To her the worst thing was that these animals did not know why she was doing this to them. With practice she may have become more adept but the business revolted her and she hung the traps up loose in the hut and left them.

As long as she needed the comfort of Magi's spiritual presence she stayed in Magi's hut as a visitor, but gradually she began to feel at home in the woods and moved into her own stone hut that she had built.

The stream ran too fast for the winter forest to catch and hold it and the water was constantly warmed by the new water gushing out of the warm innards of the earth. Fish thrived in it and Sia learned to fish; it was easier to kill these silver-scaled things, their eyes did not reproach her, she felt no humanness in them as she had in the small mammals. She also found cress and mint growing in the stream and varied her fish diet with these greens.

There was no grain for her, no milk, nor eggs for a long time and she was often sick while her body worked to adjust to the constant unchanging diet of fish and bitter greens. Nausea and diarrhea wracked her body violently for hours and she was left exhausted, empty and longing for a bowl of warm milk. She learned to fast every three days and drink large quantities of the good water fresh from the spring. She became very thin on this diet and very muscular as she still cut and carried the wood for her carving.

Eventually she too lost all traces of her sex and she was grateful for this further anonymity even in the vast emptiness around her. Like a wild animal, she feared human beings. Some days, when the air was very clear and a wind carried sound far, she thought she heard human voices, sometimes laughter, and this froze her heart within her and left her trembling and dizzy. She listened as carefully as the wild animals to the sounds of the forest, analyzing them, the speed and weight of a step on the leaves, animal or man?

At night she dreamed of snuffled breathing just outside the door of the hut. She'd lay awake, listening and hardly daring to breathe herself. It was a primitive fear of the dark perhaps that transformed the familiar forest of her days into the foreign frightening limbo of her waking dreams. And this despite the fact that all the worst, most violent things she had seen in her life had happened in full daylight. It was perhaps the mind's way of casting mystery over the most terrifying things, a buried urgent desire to not admit the mundaneity of terror and violence, the everydayness of it, and therefore the possibility of terror and violence during one's day. And so, in spite of past experience, Sia went through the ritual of fear during the night and relief at dawn.

Chapter III

In the spring the stream flooded, growing as wild and turbulent as a large river, and wrecked the homesteads built too close to its banks. In the havoc, animals ran into the forest and were lost and in this way Sia acquired some chickens and a young cow about to calf. The chickens roosted in the trees safe from foxes and Sia searched the woods each morning for eggs, sparse at first, becoming more frequent as the weather warmed. The cow made do with the meadow grasses less than an hour's walk away. There was clover there and a variety of wild flowers. But Sia would have to find a source for grain before winter if she was to maintain these animals and enjoy eggs and milk.

She understood why Magi preferred to live off wild things when she thought of all the time it would take from her carving. Still she became attached to the cow with her great liquid brown eyes. In the absence of human sounds, the cackling of the chickens and the cow's occasional sounds became like speech. She seemed to understand it as such. The cow particularly seemed to develop personality. After Sia had guided her to the meadow to graze and back to the stream to drink and then to the shelter of the forest, she began to go through the routine herself and to forge her own path through the woods.

The cow was young Sia could tell. Her udder was so small it was barely visible under her bulging body. She was in fact, still a heifer, and the calf would be her first. When the time came she was completely quiet and bewildered, even frightened and Sia could tell something was wrong. Something about the way the head and one hoof just stayed there while the mother heaved and pushed and struggled with this bewildering discomfort. Sia remembered watching a man, an uncle, when she was a child, pushing the head of a calf back inside its mother and reaching up inside the mother up to his shoulder to grab the front legs and pull them out. Sia was small and she didn't know what to feel for. She pushed hard to get the head back inside the cow but she couldn't find the other hoof. Somehow the leg was tangled inside the mother and Sia couldn't find it.

She didn't know what to do. So she prayed and waited to see if things would work out right the second time. The heifer pushed instinctively and the head came out again, wrapped in wet, grayish membrane, the long lashed eyes closed. The head with the single hoof close against it looked dead, or perhaps it felt dead. Sia felt the deadness, the heaviness of the vibrations in the air around them. The heifer tried to rub it off against a tree, backing over and over into the tree and then trying to run, she fell heaving and hot onto her side.

Sia tied a rope around the dead calf's head and hoof and then wound it once around a tree and pulled. She pulled so hard she was nearly lying on the ground but held up by the rope and still the calf would not come loose. All that day Sia tried, stopped to rest, to cry, to pray and all that day the heifer died. It took hours and hours and a great deal of effort, but by dark the heifer was dead, the head and single hoof of her calf still protruding.

All this took place on the edge of the meadow a good walk from the hut. Sia was too tired to feel the despair of all this death and she walked back and slept. In her sleep she cried; she was awakened by her own crying, surprised by it and then slowly she realized the pain she felt at the death was the pain of the mother and child, that the heifer and her calf were indeed a mother and child. And she thought about Magi and the nuns and the starving children and hysterical fathers and mothers and wondered why all living and all dying was so filled with pain and, remembering the small trapped animals, with bewilderment and misunderstanding. She saw life itself as the trap and all of them were being clumsily battered by God and none of them knew why.

In the end it was just as well she didn't have to feed the cow over the winter. She might not have been able to, and starving took longer and was more painful even than that terrible death Sia had fought on the edge of the meadow. Still Sia had to acknowledge her sorrow for the dead mother and she carved very carefully a cow in wood. When she had finished, she didn't like what she had done and she burned it immediately, though she should have waited until she needed the warmth, she was so impatient to destroy it.

In the flames there were faces, deformed faces that wavered and grew and glared at her, real faces in fact of Magi, the nuns. One by one they reproached her, hated her with their faces because she hadn't cared for them. She knew it was true and felt guilty and to make amends, she began, the next day to recreate them in wood. One by one with a rope, the rope she disentangled from the dead and bloody calf, crawling now with insects and smelling badly, she pulled the aged logs for the life-size figures to the ruined convent courtyard.

She rolled and tilted the logs into upright positions in the granary and then chose the one from which she would extract the figure of the abbess. The abbess had been the most beautiful and was closest in appearance to the idealized women Sia had always carved, like the faces and figures that Magi had carved. It was easy, a matter of habit. But the next one was an ugly nun. Sia hadn't realized that this sister was ugly, she had been good natured and sweet, but carving her features accurately into the dead wood, Sia felt ashamed that she could not capture the friendly compassionate look she remembered seeing somewhere behind the eyes, and the smile that had hidden ugliness in the flesh only intensified it in wood. The woman looked ridiculous and empty headed and Sia nearly burned this statue also.

For the first time she cursed the wood that would not bend to grace imperfection. She cursed perfection. But after dreaming of the living woman, she woke feeling more kind to herself and learned to live with the lifeless stare, layering it over with memories until she could contemplate this statue with affection. And she learned to work more slowly, more contemplatively, as in the beginning when she was first learning to carve. Sometimes she waited for dreams to guide her, dreams of the woman she was trying to immortalize. And often she spent several days contemplating the work she had done and waiting for its effect on her, its message, before she continued.

She moved back into the convent for this work and walking around, slowly, caressing the stone walls, brought back little events and overheard conversations, things she had paid little attention to the first time around. It was a kind of research and very difficult, reading all these things through a fathom of water. It was tiring and often frustrating trying to bridge the chasm between the vaguest of memories and the harsh reality of wood. Slower and slower and more carefully she worked and she began to be almost satisfied with her nuns, adding one more to the courtyard collection each fall.

All these years as she worked on memorializing her dead sisters, she spoke to no one, hiding when she thought human begins were approaching as they sometimes did en route from one town to another. She continued to live off the fish and greens of the stream and then she began to be provided with other foods, flour and oil and wine and grains. These were laid as a kind of offering at the feet of the statues that were recognizable as the murdered nuns.

Sia ate better and thrived on her solitude and silence and worked year after year until all but one of the nuns was reincarnated in wood. It never occurred to her to carve a figure of herself, nor did she know what she looked like. She was too absent-minded to examine her own reflection in the water in her bucket, though she often thought of doing it late at night when she awakened from some dream of childhood.

The convent in various stages of ruin or decay was an interesting maze and Sia felt safe within it for there seemed to be so many hiding places. She could hear people coming in to lay their offerings of grain tied in bunches at the feet of the statues and she would stand tensely waiting for the voices, whispers, and the careful footsteps to recede. It was possible these visitors were as afraid of her strange presence as she was of theirs.

One evening a half dozen people, townspeople, richly dressed and traveling with horses, came noisily into the courtyard, calling loudly to each other and exclaiming about the statues, wooden statues standing in the midst of what had obviously been the site of a large fire. And there was still food at their feet. But these sophisticated people were not interested in the symbolic portent of what they saw, but in the artistry and beauty of the work. And they began to search the premises for someone to explain. Who had done this obviously new work, and where might they find that person?

Sia tried to understand but she had become accustomed to listening to the quality of sounds, not the meaning of individual words. She found herself unable to properly listen to what they were saying; her mind's rhythms could not adjust to the rhythms of their speech. She gathered, though, that they were interested in her work and she overcame her fear to approach them. She didn't actually speak and they seemed to assume she was a mute. When the question came up of who did the carving she indicated herself in the most subtle of gestures and they requested her to come to their town with them and decorate their house with carved statues of wood.

A simple shake of her head would mean her refusal and they would go away and leave her to her peace but she remembered something long forgotten, a few words of one of Magi's rare speeches, a few words only, but conjuring up many pictures, of being a child in a town and an old man carving the apostles in stone on a church that was being built there and how this man taught her to carve in stone even before she had began to carve in wood. Surely that man would be dead now, but Sia wasn't reasoning in terms of ordinary time, she had lost track of her own time completely. Somehow she thought she would find that man, Magi's teacher and therefore to be revered, and with the money these people would surely pay her, she would buy stone and carving tools and then she would come back here and carve the stone of the ruined convent. She would carve a stone world for her oaken nuns to inhabit.

This was rash for Sia. All these years she had hidden from people and would never have dared to ride, as Magi had done, in a peddler's cart to town to trade her work for money and goods, however badly she may have felt the need. She had the vaguest memories of a town, visited twice yearly with her grandmother when she was a child, and those bits and pieces of pictures of crowds, of markets and large buildings, cobblestones and carts were mingled with the admonitions of the cautious grandmother and the purely imagined pictures of all the evils to be encountered in town were one not careful and strictly obedient. Now she simply mounted the mule they provided for her and rode with them into the foreign feared land of many people.

She took nothing; she had nothing to take; only the tools she could carry in her hands and the clothes on her back, shamefully ragged and dirty. Blending in with the forest, she was not aware of her appearance, but contrasted to these rich townspeople she couldn't help but notice that she looked every bit as frightening as had Magi when she first saw her in the woods. Of course these people were not frightened of Sia; they might feel disgust or pity or derision toward her, but even that they stifled because they desired her skill and for a price they could have it. For a price they could have anything.

She didn't think about this or resent it, she was thinking about stone and Magi's childhood, trying to imagine what it would have been like to have been Magi. She may as well have been Magi, her own history; the earliest past before she entered the convent was completely severed from her, as one day from another by the night. She felt no emotional ties to it nor even remembered it except in colorful dreams like moving stories that entertained her in her half sleep.

As the mule carried Sia through the woods she watched the trees move past her, it was as if the forest were moving and she herself were still. She watched the myriad patterns of bark and of leaves, small and crowded and overlapping but separate, each leaf outlined in the light. She watched the light and the wind and stream below moving past her and the laughing, talking voices ahead of her fell into the forest's rhythm, blending with the sounds that she was more accustomed to so that she became accustomed to them as well and everything soothed her and she never felt a moment's fear until they actually came within sight of the town.

Then a panic grew inside her so strong she almost spoke out or groaned. But she couldn't speak to these strangers and she didn't know how to go back alone. Though she had merely to follow the same winding road past the farms and through the fields to the edge of the forest, she couldn't do this alone, pass those farms unprotected by the mule and the small crowd of travelers, even disguised as she was by her rags and time, she felt like a young nun exposed and recognizable as the one who had escaped the slaughter during the famine.

She felt all this as a pain in her stomach not as a reasoned verbalized thought. Surely if she had thought about it she'd have reminded herself of the significance of the grain offerings at the statues' feet, but then that was meaningless, a superstition at a time when grain was plentiful and so was the fear of hell. When hell came back to earth as it sometimes did in times of famine and war, then indeed she would be just another helpless woman alone on the road or in the convent or in the forest, wherever she happened to be found by the enraged sufferer.

Approaching the town, they heard the faint strains of singing; the same singing Sia remembered hearing nightly when she walked through the woods from Magi to the convent. Male voices mingled with female, in song, not struggle, singing and answering, Sia closed her eyes and tried to move herself through time past the trauma and fear to the time of peace and quiet pleasure in music. She closed her eyes and let the rhythmic jolting of the mule and the distant voices sooth her her.

When finally they stopped at the house she was as if awakened from a trance and completely calm. They gave her clean clothes, men's working clothes, and showed her to a small cell-like room partly below the ground. A servant brought a bucket of water and left. After allowing sufficient time for the stranger to wash and dress, the servant returned to show her (him? the woman did not rightly know) the way to the kitchen where she had meat for the first time in many years. The meat was good and Sia smiled as she ate, slowly, and the servant, quite a young girl, decided that Sia must be a woman, a very strange, very old woman. She smiled back.

Chapter IV

Sia's year in the town seemed as long a period of time as the eleven she had spent carving in the convent courtyard, slowing down her time in order to study the previous decade. And that decade of her young womanhood had slowed as well in the routine of the convent and carving with Magi in the forest and the intense contemplation of a past that was not quite her own, not quite within her memory's reach.

Here, within the space of a half mile, she could go many places and see many people, doing business, making love, quarreling working. Sia watched all this and assimilated the faces of joy, despair, wickedness and innocence, consciously storing these faces in her memory to recreate in wood and stone. For her employers she carved two tall and lovely women at either side of the entrance to their home. When she was finished she carved a series of wood panels around the walls depicting the scenes of commerce she observed in the town. They were delighted with this work and she was totally absorbed and interested in it.

Her employers discovered that she could speak but did not often choose to do so and they paid no more attention to this particular eccentricity than they did to her strength, so surprising in such a skeletal body, or to the ambiguity of her sex. To them all that mattered about Sia was her skill in carving and in this they understood her perfectly for that was all that mattered to Sia herself. Her feelings seemed remote from herself as she herself became totally absorbed by the figures that she carved, as if she could feel no more than the wood or stone.

While Sia continued to work on the wood panels in her employer's large and impressive hall, she paid visits to the Cathedral where dozens of imaginators (what the stone workers were called) worked inside and out. They were decorating the building with the stern stone saints carved in limestone, biblical scenes populated with smaller alabaster figures carved in wood. One day Sia thought she saw the figure of a sly fox dressed in a friar's outfit preaching from a pulpit to a congregation of geese. Later she couldn't remember if this were her own imagination envisioning the work in the wood. She went back but could not find it and could not get close enough to make out the other carvings accurately.

Each of the several workers had his stove near at hand that he kept burning red-hot sending a film of rosy heat around the cathedral so that its solidity shimmered and fell in waves of hallucination. Into these stoves the men would place their tools periodically as they wore down and had to be re-ground, re-sharpened and re-tempered, often as frequently as once every hour. So immersed were they in their work that no voice rose above the unending dialogue between metal and stone.

When she had done all that was needed and wanted at the home of her employers they paid her and offered to take her back to the forest but Sia was fascinated with the activity at the Cathedral and preferred to stay. She used her wages to rent a room over a tavern in a narrow street near the Cathedral and one day, at last, she walked through the maze of stone dust and fire and mesmerized workers to find the overseer of the work, the teacher, to offer her services in exchange for instruction.

The man was young, surprisingly, extremely young and very serene. She would see him at other times pacing in anxiety when he was not immersed in the work of the carving of the saints, but in the midst of the fires he seemed alone and at peace, giving advice and instruction slowly and kindly as if no deadline existed or mattered. And indeed there was no deadline, for the hierarchy of priests that commissioned the work changed over the years while the work went on at its own measured pace. Men died and others took their places while no one doubted that each eternal stone saint would be finished and others would be started.

The young man inherited his job from his teacher, perhaps the same teacher who had sent Magi out into the forest with her salvation. For this art was truly salvation, a reason to live, to endure as long as one was needed. By chipping into the stone, the man tapped into a million years of history and worked with his short-lived hands a change in the earth itself, uniting with its eternity.

In the beginning Sia did no carving herself. She sat by the young master, grinding and sharpening and heating and cooling his tools. Sia worked on one set while he wore down another so he suffered no break in his concentration. Before her amazed eyes he carved an old woman's veined hand through a piece of fabric draped over it and put the sorrow of wisdom in her marble eyes. Only the master carved the precious marble, the most perfect, the most pure of the stones used at the Cathedral.

When he had finished the old woman he took Sia with him to the quarry a day's journey away to pick another block for his next project. He walked among the blocks of marble, some gorgeously colored, but these he ignored. He explained to Sia that the same forces that had caused the beautiful veins of color in the stone also caused hidden cracks and flaws that would be revealed after the carving was started and ruin the work. He stared at the perfect pieces as if seeing figures already hidden inside them and then he pounded them with a mallet listening intently for the high pitched sound of a flaw. She watched him water and sand and water the stones and finally make his selection. She watched while holes were drilled at intervals in straight lines around the huge block of perfectly white marble.

Into the holes were hammered wet wooden pegs. Over the next few weeks as the pegs dried and fell out, the marble itself separated and a workable piece was ready for them when they returned. The heavy marble was levered and rolled into a kind of rope cradle that swung in a wood cage on large thick rollers. It took them two days to maneuver the marble back to the city and when they camped by the road that night, Sia experienced an unusual silence and darkness for the first time in what must have been a year and a summer. One of the other apprentices had accompanied them and he sang the entire way, a strange almost tuneless chant that soothed her soul as did the velvet darkness of the night away from the many torches of the town. She longed for her home in the woods but she knew she had another year before her in the town to learn the stone carving art and she felt patient, confident that she would return. She had not yet begun to dream of Magi.

In the morning when they resumed their march with the marble toward home, her teacher told her about different stones and what it was like to carve them. He had carved small figures in a translucent amber resin that was brittle but soft to carve. One had to be very careful not to let large bits break off. It was like working with the white pine that Sia had begun with when Magi taught her wood-carving. And there were stones of many colors, not streaked like the marble, but solidly colored in bright green or purple, blue or yellow. He had traveled on both sides of the sea to find these exotic stones. He had even carved the grim gray granite which was the hardest of the stone. It was not really like carving at all but a battle with the stone as the man crushed and ground the substance down, pulverizing the granite crystals, working first with the grain and then against it.

It made Sia think of her life, every simple thing made difficult and slow by isolation, but the accomplishment sweeter for the pain of the process.

She never doubted that she would live as long as she needed to finish her work.

Back at the cathedral the master set her to work carving a figure in limestone. He let her wander among the stones and pick the one that spoke to her and asked her what she saw. She saw Magi with flowers in her hands and vines growing up along the folds of the robes over her legs. She carved Magi as a young woman, removing layers of mature personality and experiences as she stripped away the outer layers of the limestone, uncovering the skeletal remains of shellfish and small animals that had been pressured and burned into the body of the stone.

As she worked to transform the stone into a semblance of organic life, Sia endured visions and tactile hallucinations she could not explain but which spread the warmth of familiarity around her. The continued battering contact with the mineral crystals seemed to spread up through her own blood and she felt herself metamorphose into a moving mass of crystalline structures, her very blood replaced with a dense rainbow of amethyst, jasper and agate. Sometimes she felt enshrouded in a thick, heavy heat while inside she was exploding in colors and light. She felt like a star. She felt curious and frightened. She looked at her work expecting it to dance or speak. It's quiet, eternal facade of passivity disappointed her.

The room at the back of the tavern was noisy and the customers stayed later in the winter months when the difference between the day and night was blurred in the overcast skies, the cold and the general depression. There was no longer a need to rise with the dawn to work the gardens or catch the freshness of the morning. The town was covered with a shallow covering of dirty snow and even the sunsets were colorless.

Sia had trouble sleeping and began to fear sleep because of her nightmares, the noise of the tavern drifting in and out of her dreams distorting them and inspiring her sleep with terror. Frequently, she didn't know she was in these dreams, being several different people in the same dream, knowing, feeling she was this one or that one, until she had to force herself to wake up to put an end to fear and confusion. Most of the time she dreamed she was Magi.

She struggled between terror and curiosity and finally gave in to her need to know her old teacher who never spoke, and trusted the reality of her dreams. She had been learning to carve the fantastic animals and demons, as these grotesque figures appealed to the taste of the times and these strange creatures populated her dreams as well, poking out of trees or streams to laugh at her when she was most afraid, but their laughter frightened her more as she did not understand it. There was something pitiable about them even as they were so demonically ugly and malicious. The total illogic of the dreams made them difficult to remember and she was always left with vague feelings and frustrations. Then one night she dreamed the long saga of Magi's early life. It seemed to last for several days, though when she woke it was still night and customers were still laughing and brawling in the tavern.

It began with Sia as herself carving the stone of the Cathedral and she was young again and dressed in the clothing of the convent. Young men came, surrounded her and mocked her but not gently as the teacher, they mocked with cruelty waiting to goad her, to attack her and then they did attack her and then she realized that they were no longer at the Cathedral but in a dirty little side street transported there by dream time and they raped and beat her endlessly shouting her name, shouting obscenities, laughing, laughing. She struggled to wake but another part of her was watching and wanted to know what would become of Magi. The pain wouldn't stop, she had to wake, but she only dreamed of waking and then dreamed of dreaming again, a new and different dream but part of the same story. It was another place and time but she knew in her dream that it was related.

She was in the woods now and had just given birth to a baby. Her memory of the recent pain of the birth was mingled with her still vivid memory of the pain of the rape. She held the baby and looked at it once, seeing that it was grotesque like the demons and she calmly drowned it in the stream. It seemed natural to be doing this but then Sia awoke with a terrible dread in her heart. She was fully awake now and in a panic because it was too late, the baby was dead and she had killed it and she was desperate to undo what she had done. It took several minutes for Sia to realize that she had dreamed the drowning, to realize that what she took for a human baby in her dream couldn't possibly have been a human baby but was the fable character she had been carving earlier in the day and even then, realizing all this she felt overwhelmed with guilt.

She sat up all night staring at the candlelight outside her window and listening to the brawling noises of the tavern and the street, these things hypnotized her, perhaps she slept, sitting up, swaying slightly and dreamless with an enveloping feeling of guilt and panic. At dawn she went to the Cathedral not to work but to hear the mass. There was a small crowd of souls around the priest chanting and singing, looking mostly poor and all stricken, their frenzies confined within the mathematical limits of incantation, the myriad voices sublimating their chaotic suffering in perfect symmetry... mea culpa, mea culpa... mea maxima culpa.

As Sia finished her carving of the young Magi it seemed that the statue spoke to her through the mind of an ancient god, earth itself, breathing through the stone. Images played out before her as the stone took its planned shape effortlessly. It had become a well traveled road for her.

Magi left the town that had witnessed her humiliation and suffering with mockery and stayed in the forest long enough to give birth to and destroy the child. When she returned she came dressed in men's clothing and was stronger from surviving in the wilderness all those months. She no longer talked to anyone and moved silently and purposefully through the narrow streets. No one noticed her now. There was a stranger who arrived about the same time Magi returned and he was a stone carver who offered to carve the figures of the saints for the Cathedral that was always in the process of construction. When apprentices offered themselves, Magi was among them and still no one noticed her except the master who saw in her a skill as surely as he envisioned the souls of the saints in the stones he chose from the quarry. The others he set to routine and simple tasks but to Magi he taught all he knew.

As Sia carved the young Magi, the old Magi worked right alongside her, willing her to know what was in her mind, her very memories. Sia felt the alarming thrill of crushing the weak and tender throat with her strong sculptor's hands, surprisingly tender for such a large and well-muscled man. Magi felt no fear of being caught and barely cared to act secretly and yet, no one noticed her although there was so much talk about the murdered man. Ultimately, he was not much missed, having been a brutal bully and a terror in the town. She didn't remember the others, whether four or five, only the first, the surprise at the weakness of the throat. Then nothing. She had finally exorcised the demons of those men. Her teacher somehow knew and the day came when he told Magi that she was no longer safe in the town. She knew where she would go and she would create beautiful statues every day of her life to make amends for the baby.

Chapter V

Sia took her tools and left without saying anything to the young teacher. She had learned her way around the town and found the gate that let out on the road that led to her forest, her home in the ruined convent. She followed the road with her eyes downcast, not daring to look at other travelers or acknowledge their greetings. It took longer on foot and though she started immediately after the early mass it grew dark before she reached her destination. She would not stop. She walked on in the dark, feeling out the road until her eyes became accustomed to the pure, moonless dark of the chilly night. It was autumn again and very clear with a sky full of stars. Her fear subsided and the sound of the crickets made her happy and the slight chill invigorated her.

Sia gave no thought to what she might expect to find at the convent until she actually arrived there. Then she felt a disappointment that there were no fresh offerings of food and wine. In fact animals had been in to eat the grain and left their droppings in puddles of wine and oil spilled when they knocked over and broke the containers. More troublesome was the fact that one of the statues had been knocked over, the nose was broken and the entire face seemed knocked awry. It could very easily have been the animals, most probably was, but Sia felt the human hand of malice in the wreck and was disturbed and frightened by it.

Only after she had set it upright and examined the various chipped spots and thought about what she might do to repair it did she notice that one other statue was completely missing. The beautiful abbess was gone from the collection. Whether she adorned some peasant's hut, warding off evil with an eternal gesture or had been put to use warming the home, hacked to bits and consumed in flames, Sia could not know. But she took the sign to start once again with the abbess, working this time with the stones tumbled from the ruined convent.

This time the abbess would be seated in order to accommodate her shape and size to the shape and size of the available stone. There was no marble here. Sia carved in granite. Although she understood that she should sleep and eat before she began her work, she was too eager and set about to start at once. Once it was begun in the gray dawn hours she warded off hunger and exhaustion to work. When darkness came she was forced to stop but didn't sleep and continued on like this until she reached the point at which she recognized her subject and could see clearly the way to proceed. Then she went to the stream to wash, to fish and to sleep, lulled by the sound of the water. When she awoke, she was still too tired to work but felt rested enough for a walk so she decided to wander around the woods and to think about her experiences, calm now and able to look at everything, even her nightmare, with detachment.

Sia busied herself gathering herbs. She gathered what Magi had gathered and used the herbs the way Magi had used them, eating what Magi had eaten, using others as cures for cuts or rashes and hanging some in the hut to ward off evil. There was one she had seen Magi partake of only once. Sia had looked back for some reason now forgotten and had been struck by the look on Magi face, an expression of devotion and fear she would never forget.

She now decided to try this herb as well, though it had never tempted her before. She boiled it in water and drank the infusion. When her stomach reacted ominously she laid herself down in the stream to die for it was in the stream that she desired to die. She lay there a long time while the soothing water calmed her pains and she thought she must have fallen asleep and dreamed because she began to perceive the world differently. Things that shouldn't move, did move: closer and closer to her as she watched them growing in magnitude, and she felt herself disintegrating into them, into leaves or bark or water. Light and dark took no mass so that shadows seemed as real, more real, than the objects casting them. The divisions between objects became lost or changed and her gaze transformed the universe into an unfamiliar system of geometrics. Leaves were suspended from above by solid shafts of light and the trees grew horizontally along the ground in the paths of their shadows.

Sia got up and was afraid to walk into shadows, feeling the tactile hallucination of collision. The shadows were as walls to her and she stayed in the stream, not knowing where she could safely walk. Breezes she could not feel caused the smallest weeds and wildflowers to tremble and then she could not remember if she had seen their trembling or felt it and it seemed important to her to remember. She began to cry and then she slept. She could tell the difference between her visions and her dreams because her dreams were completely fantastic and impossible whereas her visions had been merely confusing. In her dreams the leaves and trees disappeared completely and returned in different places. And there were no longer the reds and golden greens of early autumn but fantastic colors she had seen in books and some on the painted statues in the Cathedral, some colors she had no names for.

Sia flew, or rather swam, through the air running away from someone who called her name and seemed alternately friendly and vicious and sometimes they both turned into stone and struggled to move through the stone or to carry it with them and all the feelings she felt, she knew for certain that her pursuer felt also in the same degree and at the same time. But she knew she was not her own pursuer. And then in her dream she fell asleep, into a deeper sleep, dreamless except for the knowledge that she didn't dream, except for the knowledge of darkness and quiet and rest.

Sia woke free of hallucinations but she could feel things before she touched them and enjoyed a greater clarity of vision. She felt enormously rested and went back to her carving and she worked well, feeling the pulsation even of stone and imprinting her mental image accurately onto the stone without resistance. After having ignored God for so many years, she now praised God for sending her strength. She began to mumble to herself the prayers that had once been the accompaniment to her life. All her walking moments she mumbled and chanted, keeping her voice to a whisper, not daring to intrude her voice on the forest's own sounds, not daring to stop her litany of praise, of apology, of supplication.

She gathered more of the herb and hung it in the door, looking at it, touching it often, not yet daring to partake of it and all the time telling herself that God had urged her to eat it and when God urged her again, she would eat it again and would open her mind to his visions. She did not try to fathom the sense or meaning of it, she expected to be shown, to feel it suddenly and be overwhelmed with it. She did not know that she was lonely. God became her friend, and her prayers, formal and musical, gave way to conversations, incessant and desperate chatter.

Sia worked quickly on the first of the planned dozen statues, working off the energy left over from her experience with the drug. And she dreamed often of the abbess. In her dreams the beautiful woman, arrested at the height of her beauty in middle age, came to Sia the young novice and praised her, befriended her and occasionally made tender and voluptuous love to her. She remembered these dreams vaguely and they made her happy. Sometimes she felt the presence of the abbess so strongly she talked to her instead of God. But the abbess had been a holy woman; where she led, even in dream, Sia's conscience left her free to follow. She felt now a trio of personalities, herself, old and solitary, the abbess of course, and then again herself as young again, re-planning her life in the safety and security of the convent. It did not matter that these were impossible fantasies, they gave her pleasure and society of a sort.

After creating the imaginary companions she allowed her real self to become a mere spectator of their conversation and activity. She slept more and sat thinking, dreaming or watching her dreams dream themselves and she carved less. Sometimes she reproached herself for slackening her work and finally she decided it was time to try the magical herb again, to see what it would do to her. Again the world become confused in her new vision but she remembered even in the drugged state that this was a kind of deception and she was not afraid to walk into shadows, afraid perhaps in a physical sense, but made brave by reason.

She sat through the initial pains and then wandered around the forest exploring the new world superimposed over the old until she fell asleep somewhere. Awakening, she would have to find her way back to the convent and sometimes this was difficult for she traveled slower through this real world than she did through her fantasy one. But she never seemed to tire or get frustrated and when she found her way back she would work with energy and ease on the stone. At the feet of the seated abbess she carved several of the small demon-like creatures her teacher had shown her, as well as leaves that coiled on vines up around her legs to lay in her lap.

The abbess herself retreated into the forest and the fantasy, hiding beneath layers of visions. Sia grew silent again, listening now all the time to the conversation of the abbess and of the young nun who was herself of the past, but growing more and more into the present and different, a personality totally different. Sia planned to carve her next. Together they went through the ritual of eating the herb. It was winter now, and they crushed the dried herb and brewed it in a tea and drank it facing each other over the fire. And they multiplied around the fire until a crowd of women went out together into the forest, leaving their tracks through the newly fallen snow. Sia felt them fanning out from her sides like angels in pictures and heard their singing faint as though from a great distance although she knew they were right beside her and in her and they moved as one.

Snakes that slithered through the snow did not frighten her because she knew that in reality they were sticks and fallen branches of trees but she delighted in the momentary sensation of terror they produced in her, in all her selves, rippling through her, the sensation. Approaching fearlessly the large fantastic shapes of bears, of dark, deformed human beings, she touched the convolutions of bark, decayed tree stumps and upended root systems, vine-covered boulders or perhaps nothing at all, her hand reaching farther and farther into shadow. The great weight of twenty years of constant fear was lifted from her as she became the master of her created world. She was totally a part of its rhythm and texture; she was safely absorbed into it.

The autumn that year had been unusually vibrant, the stream, reflecting the reds and oranges of the trees, flowed red and the light of the sun on the water reflected back onto the undersides of the leaves and all this light burned through the forest in a great liquid fire. The leaves had barely time to drift to the ground in graceful wind-dancing flights, mingling with the flocks of small blackbirds when the bare branches were outlined in snow. The snow fell continuously, softly, for several days until everything was covered thickly, soft and white and the stream itself was dappled with the small mounds of snow traveling and slowly melting along the gray current.

Sia made constant rounds through these scenes watching their changing lines and colors through the filter of greater clarity induced by the herb infusion she drank almost daily now. She ceased to carve altogether, thinking it more important to observe and praise the ever-changing sculpture of the world, or perhaps not thinking at all. She lost all sense of time; each season was its own eternity and each seasonal change a delightful surprise. She was content to be cold as she often was, and content to be hungry as long as she could watch the magic around her. She no longer desired to reduce what she saw to the single element of stone or wood or even to touch it from the outside with her hand. She had become a part of it, her hand was part of it, and together they all moved, there was no stillness to suffer the touch of her hand.

The snow melted after the magical white winter and the spring rains came and the quiescent springs in the earth flowed freely now, forming streams and waterfalls over the stones. Moisture saturated the black bark of the bare trees and soon a lace of pink and white and red and pale green blossoms erupted around them. Sia had become even thinner, rarely eating at all, and she never went back anymore to the convent where the stone abbess sat splendidly finished and alone among the oaken nuns. She wandered dazedly through the woods in widening circles, sleeping on the ground, sometimes staring for hours at the water, growing younger and younger back into childhood, back into silence.

One day she looked up from her wandering to see the apparition of a large black bear staring back at her. She had only heard of bears and seen pictures of them. Hearing her in the forest, bears must always have taken themselves out of the way of an unknown danger and she had never before actually encountered one. This animal stared through her and seemed to will her to look around at something behind her. She saw behind her the cub. For a moment the vision frightened her but she told herself she had no need to be afraid, she had moved through and demolished strange visions and shadows for many weeks and she knew that these shadows could not hurt her.

She began to move and the bear moved, but did not disappear or alter shape. Sia became confused. She began to retreat toward the cub and then the mother bear was upon her in one long quick step. Sia was enveloped in the warm, wet animal fur and the odor of the nursing mammal and her own blood gushing out of many wounds she could not distinctly feel or locate. The bear made quiet grunting noises, seemed to be speaking to the cub and Sia could hear them, but blood blinded her and she couldn't see where they were. Finally, the silence told her they had gone. She thought she should get up and try to find the convent, water and wine and some dried leaves to apply to her wounds. She thought about it a long time, but didn't have the strength to get up, and the blood flowed out with the rivulets of rain water and dew.

Sia didn't feel any pain and she was sleepy, drifting in and out of dreams for what seemed a very long time. A face, seen through a fathom of autumn red water falling and reflecting the light and shimmering on the breeze blown leaves, a face kissed her lightly on the lips and whispered and vanished. Sia got up to follow, her body light and fragmented, both gliding through the air and lying on the wet, warm earth. She struggled to run through a long dark tunnel and felt the weight of bodies against her, a crowd rushing in the opposite direction, she felt their weight and movement but saw no one. Then she heard a roar through the tunnel coming closer, louder and then receding, the sound perhaps of the stream above her. Part of her lay on the muddy bed of the stream, part of her struggled endlessly through the crowd to the coming and going of the awful roar, and another part of her was in the woods running to its edge where the peasants had burned the trees and were preparing to plow.

The trees were statues and from the flaming stumps emerged the faces of the nuns and the merchants and artisans of the town, the drunken men of the tavern and the young stone carver at the Cathedral and all the faces she ever saw in the streets as a child and forgot as an old woman, and her grandmother's face as well, all the faces chiseled and shaped by Sia's tools and wreathed with leaves or demons with snakes coiled around them, stones embedded in the bark, clutched by the roots of trees, whorled pine hands holding stone flowers.

Magi appeared in the field attempting to plow with the dream—men clinging to her, but silent now and crying. She saw their tears from the great distance of the forest and the stream and the black, smoky, noisy tunnel. The demon baby lay beside her in the mud of the stream bed and she struggled again to get up and to lift it with her but it laughed silently and then became human and dead and Sia cried and the plowmen sang with her the magical words of confession and guilt and their voices from the great distance mingled with the roar of the river, the black, smoking monster that ran through the tunnel frightening her and then disappearing and reappearing like some memory she couldn't place. The angels fanning out from her sides and moving with her had scattered and become lost and confused in the tunnel and stream and forest and field, and she could not collect and protect them and felt all their pains and fears simultaneously.

But Sia told herself that these were only visions and they would soon vanish and she would reach her hand farther and farther into shadow, into nothingness, for all was dreams. Sia felt the sensations of terror and the heaviness of guilt, but overall she told herself it didn't matter, it was all the illusion, like the bear, brought on by the drug, and perhaps God tested her strength and her reason. Sia thought then that she sang, chanted and praised, though no sound disturbed the spring forest.

The noise of the tunnel and the stream stopped throbbing in her ears and she calmly watched the plowmen, Magi among them, a man now, working the earth, turning the black rich earth beneath them. There were no signs now of the burned stumps. The wood and the ash had bled into the earth making it rich and thick and she could dig it deep and bury Magi in it and the nuns, stone or wood, and the drowned baby, but she would do it later. She was weary and wanted to sleep or to lie and watch the plowmen. And all the faces were there in the earth and many arms reached up silently, many hands reached to hold and stop the plows, all in silent struggle. But the plows moved steadily on, folding them, the faces and hands, inexorably into the black earth.

Part 2

Chapter I

In the dream
Bloodless rootless
I wandered through a fiery day
Created once in reality for me
But not rooted in time
Not experienced with blood.
I collected specimens of molten bark
Leaves that ran through my fingers like honey
But did not burn
And yet I felt them
Their heat and softness
I remember their reality.
In the cathedral
Rootless of Christ
Bloodless of martyrs
I hold the art
Of the plucked dead flower
In my hand
Rooted
In stone
In earth
I see the brown blossom
Alive
With the livingness of change.

Sia's Journal

Sia's poems were the chronicles of a hermitess displaced in time and living as lightly as a ghost, and as invisibly, on the outskirts of twentieth century life. Through the film of modern structures and sounds she glimpsed, barely felt the radiance of a memory of a home. Her exile felt complete.

Everywhere she went she looked long and hard into the faces, trying to recall the voices. Sia was fascinated by the old women of the streets, any one of whom could have been her own mother. Dressed in shawls and men's coats and shoes, pushing shopping carts or squirreling away collections of objects beneath the bushes in the city parks, from Golden Gate Park to Central Park, these homeless women resembled one another like true sisters, members of a family long dispersed. Obese, emaciated, tall, short, deformed, strong, sometimes exotic, usually drunk, often insane, they all walked with a dignity and ferocity that hid a multitude of violations. Having survived the terrors of the night, they took over the day and barely tolerated the interlopers who had to cross their streets to assigned places in the other world. Those people in business suits assumed theirs was the only reality. Sia felt lost in the interstices of one world imposed over another.

She had a dream, over and over, about an assignation. She was supposed to meet someone important at a certain time at a certain place; the time and place varied from dream to dream. But what happened when she got to the meeting place, always a little late and therefore already anxious, was always the same. She'd think throughout the various difficulties she had in getting to her destination that, when she finally made it, there would be one person, that one important person, waiting for her, and they would recognize each other. But, in fact, when she made it, dream after dream, there were hundreds of people waiting, and she recognized none of them and not one of them recognized her. Each time she dreamed of just missing a subway or a bus, or of not having enough money for a train ticket, or of getting lost on her way to an airport or boat dock, or of being too tired to run anymore, or of forgetting where she had parked a borrowed car or of realizing that she was in the wrong part of the wrong town, she'd get more and more anxious, believing so strongly that this one recognizable person was waiting and needed her.

When Sia arrived at the cafe to do a performance reading, there was a Bach string quartet playing over the strategically placed speakers. The owner went to turn it off for her but she requested that he leave it on as background, turned down a bit. She thought it would enhance her reading. It was music, after all, that inspired her poetry. She noticed a woman come in whom she recognized from her frequent visits to the Cloisters. The woman had an expression of inward concentration and walked in such a careful, graceful way that she seemed to be mentally marking the steps of an elaborate and stately dance. Sia hesitated to begin her reading, waiting for the woman to begin dancing, but the woman sat down and ordered an espresso while she looked at Sia expectantly.

"We came to the church, the old castle,

Made our way through the vineyards, the marshes,

Across the river, the old mill.

I lingered and left the others, wandering..."

Another woman came in, rushing and clearly trying to be quiet and joined the thoughtful dancer. She whispered a few words to her friend and Sia was conscious of an incredibly deep and mesmerizing voice.

"Twisted vines cut the mist

Green and gray and brown all through the mist

The castle disappears in clouds

Covering far villages

Softening the lines, the old mill disappears

Clouds cover the hills, soften the lines

Colors run together into falling night

A solitary star...."

"Who's doing the reading? She looks familiar." The simple question was transformed into great significance by the beauty of the woman's voice. The woman tried to whisper, but who would want to quiet such a voice?

"Standing in a valley watching the hills

Move toward me

In the fast falling night,

The shadows animate the hills, trees run to me.

I hear the evening birds, the river rush,

Cars on the highway sound in the river,

Headlights animate the trees that run to me

And pass into falling night..."

"I don't know. I've never heard of her before, but I know what you mean, she does look familiar. Has she been here before?"

"No I don't think so. I'm sure I've seen her somewhere else though."

As they whispered, another slender, dark, intense looking woman came in and sat down by herself in a corner. Sia was aware of the voices, the one who recognized her the most compelling, and she was aware also of the wonderful colors and patterns in the lone woman's dress, but even as she noticed all these things, she continued to chant, imagining her own voice, deep and sensual, and feeling herself shrouded in brilliant colors and lonely grandeur.

"Lights among hills many shades of dark,

Twigs break beneath my feet, dry grass and rocks.

In the full dark night I ran with trees through the valley

and crossed the road in the glare of the highway,

 Through the gate to the warm fire inside,

The glare and voices still far in the silence,

The evening birds gone.

The place makes me sad remembering

The bus to Baltimore, trees on either side,

The road never ending, the forever dream.

The cobbled town, old,

I remember the ride forever back and forth

Between the dying leaves in the fast falling night,

Lights across the bay,

The same solitary star

And the never ending contralto of the evening birds..."

Sia became aware of yet another voice. "It was so depressing I couldn't stay. She'd saved every piece of mail she'd ever received, even the junk mail. It filled the kitchen drawers, all neatly stacked according to size. I didn't read it of course, but I imagined she'd stacked advertising brochures right along with love letters or letters telling about old friends who had gone away and died."

"Love letters?"

"Places of Longing,

To walk always with black trees in the black night,

Stars and silence in my head,

Even my own voice humming

Comes to me from far,
This music,
forget the long-ago loves that shatter the heart,
As glare and indifferent noise of now
Shatter the medieval mist,
Castles in hills, old mills and the dream river,
If I was ever there..."

"Well you're right, that does seem unlikely. But no, there could've been some really OLD love letters in there, like from the twenties maybe. I mean she saved everything, paper bags all flattened out and stacked in cupboards, plastic strawberry baskets, everything for god-sakes!"

"I am leaving
For the cities and the constant glare and noise of now,
The birds at dawn in the park,
The mist-hid houses, the medieval mist
In the car the lights animate the trees,
The forever dream..."

"How long had she lived there?"

"Oh that's the worst. She's only been there since her last husband died about six years ago. She actually moved all that stuff from her old house. It was depressing I have to tell you. I should've stayed longer but I couldn't. Suddenly all of life seemed to be empty boxes and bags and old news. It didn't seem worth living, let alone trying to get close to my mother.

"Are you alright?"

"Oh I'm fine. Very detached finally and that's very liberating. I'm going to the country, grow vegetables and flowers and nourish myself with color. I'm hungry for colors. Who is this woman that's reading?"

"Her name is Sia. I met her at the record store. She helped me find some music I'd been looking for and we got to talking. What do you think of her poetry?"

"I'm not into poetry really, but having readings is a good idea. Every other cafe has a guitar player."

"To contemplate forever the sound of the river and the old mill
Disappearing in mist,
To be 700 years old,
A Sybil in the earth,
Black loam,
A witch in flames,
The voices far away,
To hear only the leaves and dry grass and broken rocks,
Green and gray and brown,
Through the mist the dawn birds,
The silent night,
To see twisted trees black in the night,
To see the night,
Remember the silences and solitudes,
And coming into now, the medieval mist too cold,
Too long ago the valleys and paths of silence comfort me.
I live in the mists,
Remembering,
I live in fragments of landscape,
Scattered across years and secret roads."

The poem and the string quartet and the various conversations all ended together.

"Oh, I like that last line," the lovely deep voice said and the graceful woman nodded.

The owner asked Sia if she wanted him to turn the record over and she asked for something more modern which he didn't have and they decided she should read the next one unaccompanied. He brought his companion some coffee and Sia resumed, looking at the lone woman in the beautiful dress, who looked back at her. She looked familiar too, not like a face in a crowd at the museum, but like a face in a painting or sculpture Sia had once seen and forgotten.

"This is called "Song of the Highway," she said. The graceful woman nodded and her friend said, "Oh, this should be good." Sia thought such a voice should be used sparingly or it would overwhelm.

"White mountains,
Black mountains,
Mountains of car parts
And railroad cars,
Approaching south Baltimore,
Baltimore, Baltimore,
Rows of houses
And row houses
Laundry lines
Of yellow sheets
And gray sheets,
Billowed
And whipped by wind,
Trumpets articulate
Textures and colors
Of fat men dancing
In the stilted formality
Of modern vision,
The modern solutions
To mystery,
Fugues
Lost
In news
Of war,
And the blues advertising
Additives
Preparation H,
Bombs,
And preaching
Hell
In the landscapes
And dreams in the car,
Tentacles of sun
Through windows,
Music from bars
Highway singing

Lone women
On highways
In high heels
And vacant eyes
In vacant lots
And parking lots
The music of courts,
Remote and golden
Silk on the filth of old skin,
The songs of decay,
The songs of lust,
The music of mountains
Driven gray and poor,
Wails like a trapped coon,
Appalachian Mountains,
New Mexico Mountains,
Mountains of silence,
Time and space
Reel
Seen through windows
And mirrors,
Imprisoned in buses,
Imprisoned in cars,
Shot through
Time and space
And reason
Like bullets,
And coming out strangers,
Confused and frightened,
Singing
We are here
We are here
We're at the end of the highway
We're turning back now
To Baltimore, Baltimore."

The deep-voiced woman clapped and smiled with a bright flash of white teeth and black eyes, the graceful woman nodded in her sage and serious way, the woman in colors continued to stare and smiled slightly and the owner's friend who had listened without a word throughout said she did actually like that one, especially the reference to hookers on the highway.

"How do you know she meant hookers? Could've been barmaids going home or some woman who had a fight with her boyfriend and started hitchhiking."

"OK I just liked the image. Can I have some more coffee? It's good stuff. What is it?"

Sia read a couple more poems and then thanked her small audience. The owner invited her to sit down and have some coffee and quiche and introduced her to his friend Mary Anne, who had bought a small homestead in West Virginia, and, while they talked, the woman with the deep voice came over and introduced herself. Her name was Ruthie and she called herself the Queen of Chaos and talked about Tarot. She could have said anything and Sia would have considered it wise and important because of the hypnotic quality of her voice, like the muses perhaps or the sirens. That voice even made Ruthie beautiful, although seen in inanimate repose and silence, she appeared ugly. Sia would always be surprised by photographs of Ruthie.

Ruthie's friend, Lila joined them and they invited the lone woman in the colorful dress, as she appeared to be watching them. Her name was Alexandria. The owner gave her his chair and the five women talked long into the night while he cleaned up, closed, and tossed Mary Anne the keys. "Lock up when you leave" . . . . he was a tired and kindly man.

Checking the time, Mary Anne told them it would be dawn in an hour and suggested going to watch the sun rise over the ocean and they headed out to Coney Island all crowded into her ancient compact Volvo.

In winter, at night, the ocean beaches gave Sia a thrilling feeling of primitive terror and awe. She felt the eternal infinitude of all awareness when faced with the sound of waves endlessly breaking, retreating, and breaking again. It made even music seem paltry in comparison.

No one spoke, all walking slowly along the lacy edge of the wet sand and foam, each alone with her thoughts. Then Lila began to wave her arms in exquisite movement, large sweeping gestures and she took long rhythmic strides, almost, not quite dancing. Then Ruthie laughed and the sun came up and the gulls started screeching and Mary Anne waved to another friend she had spotted down the beach. The day began.

The sixth woman was Brenda, a sculptress and old friend of Mary Anne's who thought herself a photographer, though she talked more about it than she actually practiced it. It turned out that all the women created or contemplated some art form. Ruthie made quilts on commission but secretly did drawings and paintings of Native American myths, secretly, because she considered them sacred.

She told how she once painted an owl and shortly thereafter her first child was killed in an auto accident and she miscarried the second child in the same accident and she was sure she was being punished for making and displaying the image of the owl, because to her tribe, the owl was an omen of death, and she was forbidden to even look at one, much less reproduce it.

Ruthie's grandmother was a Kiowa from Oklahoma who had married an Anglo oilman, acquiring safety and wealth all at once, for it was dangerous to be an Indian. Then Ruthie's mother up and married an Apache who ran off to Africa shortly after Ruthie was born. Her mother's second husband and all her half sisters were as blonde and blue-eyed as the careful grandmother could wish, but Ruthie looked pure Indian and her grandmother couldn't help loving her best. Ruthie herself ran from wealth and safety when she was sixteen, living on the streets in Berkeley, on a commune in Colorado, riding the dog across the country, and was now visiting Lila in New York. To Ruthie, a stay of several years could still be called a "visit" because she had not yet found a place where she could feel at home. Sia looked up suddenly when Ruthie said that and almost spoke, but decided to wait.

Alexandria was also an artist, a calligrapher fascinated by medieval illuminated manuscripts. She was Jewish, the child of two parents who were each the sole survivors of their respective families. All her grandparents, aunts, uncles and cousins had died in concentration camps. She wore an antique brooch she found in a vintage store pretending it had belonged to her grandmother. She had a photograph of her father's family and the brooch looked like something her father's mother would have worn. She agreed with Mary Anne that gardening was very soothing when all else lost meaning.

Lila's mother, a Japanese woman, had been in a concentration camp too, in California during World War II, while her Mexican husband fought. He returned one-legged, and in place of his left leg he had medals. The war made him crazed. After Viet Nam this would be labeled as a specific mental illness, but then he was just another crazy violent Mexican in and out of drunken rages, in and out of jail. Lila's parents divorced when she was a baby, and her mother still lived in San Francisco where she still worked as a waitress, but her father returned to his small hometown in New Mexico, whose population consisted primarily of his second wife's family. Brenda's face lit up.

"No kidding! My Dad's family still lives in Cimarron and everybody's cousins."

"That's funny, you don't look Mexican." Alexandria ventured and they all laughed, trading parodies of racist remarks they'd all heard and calling Mary Anne the token white person. "Well my parents didn't have me until they were quite old and they were both divorced several times so that's something anyway."

Sia didn't speak of her background. She never did because she knew that however bleak someone else's childhood may have been, they'd always feel sorry for her when they heard about her mother and she hated that. She also hated lying. Somehow both situations made her feel disloyal. So Sia became adept at asking questions of others and their answers never ceased to fascinate her.

She was accustomed to these spontaneous groupings of kindred souls, and often partied and traveled and visited for days at a time with people she'd just accidentally run into. She still corresponded with some, but usually they went their separate ways and became part of the accretion of her memories and she of theirs. This time on the beach at Coney Island, shortly after dawn, she found herself included in a long-term plan to form a kind of convent in the country where the sisters would worship nature and create art. Mary Anne had recently bought some land with money her father had left her and she was leaving shortly to supervise some improvements, like drilling a well and winterizing the old shack that was on the land. Sia had no roots to hold her in the city, so she planned to join Mary Anne within the month, and the others would follow by summer.

It was early March, with a little of winter left in the air and a little of the promise of summer, and anything was possible and everything was a gamble.

Chapter II

"The geese fly in arrow formations shouting to each other, silent only when in perfect formation, hurrying to catch up, to find each its own place. They fly with determination and purpose and a certain hostility, perhaps aggressive wariness describes it better. They know about hunters, their shouts are constant warnings and commands. The small blackbirds rise up in the sky as if thrown up by the handful, and float spiraling down to the nearest branches. There is always a core of concentrated black dots, darker in the midst of the more lightly scattered dots, and as they fly, circling over a tree or cornfield, the dark core spirals inside the widening crowd, making beautiful dot patterns in the sky. Then they disperse to a wide, light sparseness and land. I'm studying the different movements of the birds not as a naturalist, I don't even know the names of all the birds, but as a sensualist, as a dancer might. A dancer could use these descriptions of motion. And the accompanying sounds. The single, distinct commands of the arrowed geese, the random dot-like sounds, short sounds running into each other and changing with the density of the small black birds. The solitary hawk that soars on the rising currents of earth-warmed air, the hawk is silent, but for a rare and lonely cry, echoing on the air in rhythm with the spiraling heat. When I am inside and hear the birds, I run out and watch them until they are gone and their echoes are silenced. I wait for every vibration to be perfectly stilled and then I go in, peaceful and rested."

Sia's journal

Mary Anne sold her forty acres in Lincoln County, West Virginia to a traveling commune at a music festival, and was driving to Monroe County to look at another piece of land with plenty of year-round springs. She carried with her the depressing sound of well drillers at work, drilling hour after hour and day after day until her money ran out, and all she ever got was a trickle of water. Other folks could live with cisterns; she craved the soothing fetal sound of constantly running water. Together Mary Anne and Sia drove Mary Anne's old truck through the hollers saying goodbye to the locals.

Sia concentrated on the scenery: the shopping mall, the railroad tracks, the dirt road through the countryside, small towns with crazy angled buildings holding each other up, and old men chewing tobacco and spitting it out at them and muttering as they passed. There were fat white women with dough-like skin and skinny and dirty children shouting obscenities to Sia's ear. It took Sia awhile to get used to the foreign speech patterns and accents of the mountain people, but as with most things, once used to it, she liked it well enough.

They turned and drove parallel to the tracks for awhile and Sia watched some boys playing on top of the coal trucks, sitting there waiting. It seemed in this place they might wait forever. Every man they saw was mostly toothless and had his enormous wad of tobacco tucked away in one cheek, completely deforming his face. The women too were mostly toothless, the young as well as the old, and they were fat, women, almost all of them, fat on potatoes and wonder bread bought with food stamps. The children and the men were skinny and wiry and looked to be strong with a strength nourished by necessity, there was nothing else.

But there were gardens everywhere, big and little patches of corn and beans and potatoes and cabbage, beside the tracks, beside the public road, behind the general store and the post office, everyone labored over their corn and beans. Sia soon learned that's what people talked about around here:

"Are the beans ready yet?" "How many quarts did you can."

"Is the corn ready yet?' Nothing like it, corn and tomatoes and new potatoes, little ones."

So and so got herself a freezer, so nice to freeze in summer instead of having to can all day over the hot wood fire, but some preferred their food canned, were used to it, didn't like frozen vegetables as well, some thought it was better, tasted better as well as being more convenient, being easier.

They talked about the weather when it happened to enter into garden conversations and politics too, in a wild, fanciful way. To these mountain folks, war with someone was always imminent, not war over there, but war over here: who would be ready for the invasion? There was a lot of speculation over America's readiness for invasion by the ubiquitous enemy, be it Russia or China or some South American "power".

Some folks came out to the truck and stood in the road to talk. Some places they stopped and got out to visit in houses. At the first house, Sia was at a loss where to sit or where even to stand, the floor boards of the porch were rotting and there were holes everywhere. The chairs and sofa looked equally dubious. They were not invited in. Apparently it was customary for folks to do their visiting on the front porch, which served as a living room. Looking inside, she discerned three rooms, a kitchen and two rooms that could have been bedrooms or sitting rooms, both strewn with useless looking furniture and piles of clothes.

The house belonged to the grandparents, and with them lived or visited nearly half a dozen children and perhaps another half dozen grandchildren, including two or three infants. It was hard to keep track in the confusion. All the young men were working on a number of cars that were parked in the yard, some on wheels; some on cinder blocks. They appeared to be taking parts from some cars and putting them in others, and once in awhile, one grease-covered, laughing-eyed boy would start up one of the cars and drive it around with a roar in the yard while the little kids screamed with mock fear and real pleasure and the young mothers of infants scolded.

The fat old grandmother sat in her chair on the porch, half sleeping and half frowning, her hands resting on her belly like a table in front of her. The grandfather was missing one eye. Sia was embarrassed when a child insisted on asking about it, but the children talked about the old man and woman, their various ailments and their age and peculiarities, right in front of them in loud voices. It may have been a game they played, expressing their festering resentments, pretending the old folks couldn't hear, but they heard, Sia could tell. Mary Anne had bought her land from them, it turned out, and they seemed to regard her and Sia as foolish young city folks. Sia couldn't help but agree.

The next family they visited was new to the county. He'd been a miner in Kentucky and came here because he'd met someone who would rent him the house and land cheap, five dollars a month. Again there were three rooms, and water was brought in from a well in buckets. They also had a barrel to collect rain water, but all kinds of things were growing in it. They had beautiful incongruous names these folks, the Greenhill family. The wife's name was Elvira. They seemed romantic, still very much in love, though both were toothless and wizened. Though she was prematurely aged with misfortune, Elvira couldn't have been much more than forty five, if indeed the infant was hers, either that or the oldest daughter at home was the mother at fifteen, either possibility it's own kind of tragedy.

Elvira was the first grown woman in the area that Sia had seen who wasn't fat, in fact she was emaciated. While the girls finished doing the laundry in the yard, stirring it in a cauldron of boiling water hung from a tripod over a wood fire, Elvira dragged out a small electric organ plugged into an extension cord that hung from the center of the ceiling and played hymns to amuse her smaller children and her guests. It was a great pleasure to them. They also had a radio, but no television. On the walls were magazine pictures of Jesus and movie stars and some presidents, Kennedy and Eisenhower.

The others they had visited along the way had all seemed inundated by their poverty, sunk in lethargy and totally at home with filth and wreckage, but the Greenhill family was gentle and oddly noble, and these qualities made them seem tragic and romantic to Sia. She would never forget them and sometimes fantasized better times for them even knowing that for Elvira Greenhill better times could only come in fantasy.

Their last visit that day was to the woman who lived down the road from the property that Mary Anne was leaving, the woman who had a phone and took messages. Sia had left her message for Mary Anne about her arrival time with Lee who was living with a man now, maybe a husband, and several children, some her own and others she had taken in. She was in the process of converting the chicken house into a dwelling for yet another orphan, a young woman who had a baby, actually, who was leaving her husband, he beat her, and she had nowhere else to go.

Lee talked fast and nonstop. Her accent was the same as all the other folks in these hollers, but her vocabulary was extensive and colorful. She had a sister married to a rich man in Florida. She had visited her sister in her mansion in Florida, but she preferred her mountains, her valley, and her cheerful, free and gregarious poverty.

While Lee talked she fed a bottle to an infant on her hip, prepared sandwiches for the other kids, showed off and fondled some chicks she was raising in the living room, got out to show and put away again the number-painting kits she sold at fairs and parties, and pointed out the paintings she herself had made for their own home. She also managed to strip a bed, put on clean sheets, and stash the old ones with a growing pile destined for the Laundromat in town. Her old man was a truck driver, made enough money for luxuries like the Laundromat and a freezer, which she kept outside in the back under a lean-to.

Despite all her activity, Lee never lost track of her narratives. Some folks drove by and shot through their window one night. Lee had a suspicion she knew who it was. Once she met that guy in the woods. She had her gun and he had his and they both pretended to have sighted a snake. There was an ominous silence which she pantomimed, the eyes, the head slowly rising from the ground, seeing first the enemy's feet, then legs, and so on up to the face, the tension and then the break, the friendly conversation between these two who apparently wished each other dead and made no bones about it. She never did say why and Sia, following her through the rooms as she talked and worked, never had the opportunity to ask.

They went outside to visit the young runaway wife who was white washing the chicken house that was to be her home for awhile. She had written letters, She was waiting to see what direction her life would take. She'd decorated the walls with maps: aerial maps, road maps, forest service maps, world maps, quadrangle maps, a state map on which one could find the names Sod, Midkiff, Branchland, Mud, Nitro, all names as if they were places like anywhere else. No one would ever dream, if they didn't already know, that in such places men still beheaded enemies and raped daughters and burned barns and rotted with filth and whiskey and drove their women old and wizened before they hit forty.

There was a brickyard, somewhere at the end of rutted and twisting roads, where one could go in the night and pick up the flawed bricks that couldn't be sold and had been cast off onto a growing mountain of hard red bricks, pick up those bricks and build yourself a fire place or a stove flue, for free. You went in the night after working hours and climbed around the dangerous, moving mountains of cast-off bricks and looked up occasionally into the glare of the furnace lights. It was like a scene from a Bosch painting in the brickyard, buried among the hills and mountains and hollers of western West Virginia, cut off from reality and struggling through your nightmares back into the inhabited world. You could find the proof of that dream on a map with the name Nitro, jumping out of the maze of letters and lines at you.

Later that night, camping in the truck, Sia felt so alive and happy she thought she would scream out and holler, Mary Anne was asleep and they had a long drive the next day. She settled for a contented smile and stared as long as she could keep her eyes open at the endless sky.

The next day they visited a patriarch named Harlan whose silent wife put biscuits and gravy and sausage and eggs in front of them while Mary Anne and Harlan competed for the title of most long-winded rhetorician in the county. Six days of the week Harlan worked demolishing old houses to make way for fast food restaurants and gas stations, and on Sunday he presided over the hillside around his house, strewn with iron gates and old windows, some with colored glass, and lumber full of nails, and claw- footed bathtubs, old sinks and toilets.

All the young people came to purchase his wares to build and furnish the shacks they contrived to put up on their land. And he would entertain them with his views and encouragement for what they were doing. His many daughters ran in and out, with babies on their hips, children of their own, or younger brothers and sisters. The generations of Harlan's family were as confused as the assortment of junk in his yard. Sia enjoyed the visit; she drank a number of cokes and used the flush toilet frequently. She sat on a collapsed sofa from which it was difficult to extricate herself and watched the flickering television in the darkened living room with a constantly changing number of women and children and listened to the strange new music of their accents.

The parade of faces reminded Sia of those carved into old and age-polished oak in the Cloisters. She was a good listener, just responsive enough to keep people talking unaware that their voices were the background music to the fantasies she cast them in. What they said held little meaning for her, how they said it told more.

From Harlan they received a hand-drawn map to the home of a couple near Alderson, who had land for sale in Monroe County. Sia compared it to the road map, fascinated by the names of places, and meticulously followed their progress, matching the reality to the busy, intricate diagram of roads and landmarks. She even wanted to stop and visit the woman's prison at Alderson, which Mary Anne thought was lunacy, knowing nobody there. To Sia all strangers had a kind of remote familiarity.

When they finally arrived at the couple's house, their headlights attracted them, and they came out curiously, wondering who could be visiting them. It was possible they preferred not to be disturbed, as they were not enthusiastic and friendly in the way some of the young people so often were. Sia was suspicious of that friendliness anyway. They weren't unfriendly either, just curious mostly, and very polite, even kindly.

The woman was beautiful with a beauty that was deeply grained and would increase with age. Sia thought she would age like the trees, each season of the year leaving some sign, and that she would live a long time. The man was slight and youthful, the years left no mark on him and because of this Sia had the premonition he would die young. It was inconceivable that he would ever age.

They stood and moved inside a small world of wood. The house was filled with finely sanded rounds of ash and cherry for tables stacked against the walls, with the legs stacked in corners until the boundaries of the work rooms grew smaller around them. And the forest grew around the house, protecting and inspiring them.

Sia admired the simplicity and unity of the environment where everything was wood, worked and un-worked, and she remembered the couple later as statues of wood themselves, frozen in postures of farewell.

Seeing them later in a crowd at the State Fair, she recognized them only as caricatures of themselves, and that memory was as of a photograph in a book, so remote and unreal did they seem outside their world of wood.

The couple drew another map for Sia, who had taken over the navigation, attempting to show its boundaries and highlights. There was a cave, a waterfall, several streams. After several tries, the young man presented them with an artistic diagram he hoped was also accurate. The couple made plans to meet Sia and Mary Anne the following week in Lewisburg, where they planned to sell handcrafted furniture at the State Fair.

The young man also carved in stone and indeed loved this work even more then his wood working, but it was the wood work that paid the bills. Only rarely did he get a commission for stone work. At the state Fair he demonstrated stone-carving techniques and answered questions from people who came to watch. Sia asked more questions then anyone. How did he begin? Which did he prefer wood or stone? Which kinds of stone? He explained to her that when he was sixteen he watched trees growing out of the earth, and that since then wood kept him grounded, steady. After he began to work in wood he moved on to stone carving, inspired by the Renaissance sculptures, awed by the work of Michelangelo. He recalled the statue of Moses, how he could see it breathe.

Later he went into the woods to work alone. He preferred stone and needed to be always working. Only when he was working did he feel peaceful, and he never got tired, even eating seemed a waste of time, but he was not impatient to finish. It was the act of carving that was more important than the result, and he was confident. He'd start a project with drawings and clay moldings, then he'd carve it in wood and finally in stone. When he could afford it, as when it was commissioned, he preferred the purist marble. He was obsessed with perfection. The deeper in the earth, the more pure the stone, he told her. Sia was fascinated that the colors she loved in marble floors were perceived as imperfections by the sculptor.

Chapter III

I collected specimens of molten bark
And leaves that ran through my fingers like honey
But did not burn
And yet I felt them
Their heat and softness
I remember their reality

Daily Sia traversed the boundaries of the land, the land she shared in name with the co-op, but actually enjoyed in solitude. She filled a black-bound book with sketches of the different kinds of barks and leaves, and notes on how the different kinds of wood burned. Locust was best. It had little leaves, several on a stem, and thorns in the summer. And its leaves turned early, they were the first reddish brown of the fall, even before the fall, in late July and early August they turned, and by fall they were gone. The locust trees became bare black lines, an etched pattern over amorphous shapes of red and gold, and the patterns of its bark were deeply etched, the roughest bark. Hickory was good, and all the oaks, but some oaks better than other, white oak burned hotter then red oak. Black oak burned better than pin oak. Sia learned to see the difference in the oaks by the striations of their barks. There were also nut trees, walnut and beechnut and even some old dead chestnuts standing in someone's long-ago orchard, and twisted apple trees that would bear well when pruned after all these years, and peach trees and cherry trees, many wild ones that grew from pits thrown out along the road and warmed by the breeze from the creek. There were groves of straight poplars, light gray bark, almost smooth and large yellow leaves dropping gracefully. There were hemlocks and white pines, but mostly there were maples, old maple trees standing brilliant electric orange against the blue autumn skies. Once the valley had been called "Sugar Grove" when there had been enough families there to support a school. The little white building still stood, and there was a church, the road to it only a deer path now.

All the co-op members had enjoyed the first summer, sleeping in the old hayloft of the barn that leaned away from the wind at a precarious angle or in tents. Ruthie had stayed in her hand-painted Tipi, for which she had cut the poles from trees on the land. Sia had simply slept on the ground, a waterproof tarp under her sleeping bag with enough left to wrap over the top when it rained. She loved to duck her head inside the warm sleeping bag, soft on its bed of old autumn leaves, and hear the rain drops hit the metallic tarp and stay dry beneath it. Sometimes she'd peek out to smell the pine and earth smells brought forth by the rain and she'd touch the wet leaves with her hand. Then she'd watch the clouds move across the sky, revealing a multitude of stars in their wake, and finally, overcome with a delicious drowsiness, she'd drift off to sleep again, all curled up in her down cocoon.

She was so immersed in the sensual pleasures of the forest and the earth that she took little notice when, one by one, the others went off on brief forays into "civilization" and then failed to return.

Originally the plan had been for each of the six women to spend two months in the city, working and sending money back to contribute to the mortgage payments on the piece of land Sia and Mary Anne had found. Those living on the land would do their best to earn what they could, working for local farmers, selling produce, eggs and milk at the health Food Coop in Roanoke, or doing part-time work in any of the towns within an hour's commute. If any of them were lucky enough to be paid for their art, those earnings would also be contributed.

Lila had left first, back to San Francisco to participate in a performing arts festival on the docks and to teach dance. When she wrote to say that she'd been accepted into a company, they were all happy for her because that was what she had always really wanted to do and they knew she needed to dance. Lila sent a check to cover one month's payment, and by the time the next payment was due, Alexandra would be able to send it from her earnings in New York.

But Alexandra "came out" that trip and fell in love and decided it was selfish to retire to the country when there was so much work to be done to achieve equal rights for all Gays and Lesbians and she needed her earnings to subsidize a newsletter she was starting with her lover. Ruthie, Brenda, Mary Anne and Sia all wished her well and thought that the four of them could manage.

Then Brenda was called to Albuquerque to tend to her dying mother who rallied and sank and rallied and sank until she couldn't afford her share either, and she wrote back with regrets that she couldn't make any payments anymore. Ruthie and Sia got orchard jobs that October and spent their days atop ladders with canvas bags slung over burdened and aching shoulders. The bags were designed with hooks on the open bottoms that could be folded up and hung on the top so the apples wouldn't fall through the bottom into the crates until the picker unhooked the bag, emptied it, re-hooked it and started all over again to fill it to back-breaking weight. Mary Anne tended the homestead and took care of their few animals until the harvest season was over and then she left for the city and started sending back money orders.

Mary Anne came back when it was Ruthie's turn to do a city stint and then the next Sia and Mary Anne heard, Ruthie was quitting her job in Breckenridge, Colorado to go traveling among the Indians of the Southwest. Then she wrote to say she'd "found herself" with the Havasupai at the bottom of the Grand Canyon and that they should sell the quilts she'd left with them and use the money to make as many payments as that would cover. She assured them the Creator would look after them.

When it was necessary for one of them to return on a full-time basis to a city job to support the land, Mary Anne, hinting at glamorous connections, volunteered to go while Sia stayed to make improvements. So Mary Anne ended up living back in New York and partying a lot, while Sia was happier than she'd ever been, making a garden, tending a cow, chopping wood and exploring the forest.

There was a three-room shack on their land that they hoped to replace with a larger, warmer stone house. The walls were like sieves, letting in rats and mice and occasionally snakes, and dust and bugs and, in the winter, the wind. There was running water from a spring up the hill, their land had several springs, all strong and pure and beautiful. In winter she had to leave the pipes running so they didn't freeze and even then they sometimes did, when the temperature dropped to five degrees and the wind blew at sixty miles per hour.

Sia didn't mind that, or the outhouse or the kerosene lamps when the electric lines went down in a storm, she didn't even mind the cold. She didn't mind those things the first year because she was hopeful about the stone house and because she was too involved with her observations of a world that was new and fascinating to her. The people of the county, the old timers, were all characters to her in an inner film and she would visit them and later record their ramblings like an anthropologist on a distant island. She took notes on the weather and the quality of the light at certain times of the day. The time just about an hour before twilight was most exciting, vibrating. She noticed the lull in March just before the winds when the nights were almost summery, reeking of rain and the earth saturated with melted snow. She filled her notebook with sketches and poems, and she was constantly excited and enthralled and didn't notice that weeks went by when she didn't see anyone.

Some Sundays Sia visited neighbors. Sometimes she went to Mrs. Bradley's and Mrs. Bradley always invited her to stay for a big dinner. It was embarrassing, she couldn't return this hospitality, but of course she couldn't offend Mrs. Bradley by refusing, and it was delightful to stay and partake of stewed squirrel, apple sauce, three different kinds of beans, biscuits made that morning (as they were every morning) on the wood cook stove, a salad of greens from the garden and plenty of onions, homemade butter imprinted with flowers, and strong coffee with fresh milk.

Even now, with just the two of them, Mrs. Bradley cooked as she did when she had eight kids at home. Two of her sons lived on their land, having put up a trailer and built a brick house, respectively and sometimes her grandsons would meander over around lunchtime. They called it dinner.

Her daughter-in-law Kathleen came over occasionally to give her a home permanent. If Sia saw her car out front she just passed on by. She didn't like Kathleen and Kathleen didn't like her. Nobody liked Kathleen much, she was a grouch and her nephews teased her endlessly to get her angry. She was famously fat and her own husband made cracks in public about it, about how if the bull got loose she wouldn't even be able to run. But Sia always had a nice enough time with old Mrs. Bradley.

Mr. Bradley was senile and sat in a rocker and interrupted now and then to ask who you were and where you lived and his wife would repeat the information for him with a weary patience. Mrs. Bradley resented being tied to the house when she was still healthy and full of energy. She wanted to go out and pick berries and go shopping in town, but she had to make sure he was safely asleep before she could even go work in the garden.

Sometimes Sia went to see the Rayhill family, two brothers who lived on the family farm with their mother, who was pushing a century, and a housekeeper. Their brothers and sisters had all married and moved away, some as far Baltimore, and John still visited his girlfriend Annie, whom he never married because his mother wanted someone to stay and mind the farm. Some asked why not bring Annie down to the farm? Well no one rightly knew, John and Annie had been a couple, an unmarried couple, for decades. Maybe she didn't want to get married, she was mighty independent,

Annie was, delivering the mail, working in town, full of stories and ideas. Maybe Annie didn't want to get married and have a bunch of kids and take orders from her husband, because that's what marriage meant in those parts even nowadays.

Sia liked Annie. She liked having dinner there with John and his widowed sister Lureen Bagby, who was always full of jokes and laughter, and Lureen's visiting grandchildren. Sitting around the Kitchen table, Lureen and Annie winked at each other, figuring out who was going to repeat the risqué joke that the young minister had told about the pickled beans one Sunday while visiting after church (Sia had brought pickled beans).

"Well there was this traveling minister (naturally the minister made a joke about a minister instead of a traveling salesman) who was to stay with a family for the night. They had pickled beans for supper and what was left over the wife put in a pot on the table. They was real good, them beans was. Well they had only this one bed, see, and the minister had to sleep with the man and his wife in the same bed. The man slept in between the minister and his wife. Well in the middle of the night, see, there was this noise like a knocking, and the wife she says to her husband "I think someone's out by the barn, better go check' and the husband he goes out and when he's out of the room the wife she turns to the minister and says "now's your chance' and the minister, he runs into the kitchen and eats up all the pickled beans!"

Much laughter and blushing, Sia loved the incongruity of it, these old Christian folks telling adolescent jokes about sex, or rather not about sex as it turns out. And then they told with indignation about the same minister asking their 98-year-old mother if she had kissed her husband before they were married, and were so proud that she had looked the young man in the eye and asked him if he kissed his wife before they were married, thereby putting him in his young upstart place. She died, the old Mommy as they still called her, before her 99th birthday in the fall.

Annie told about her friend who got a job as a housing inspector and wouldn't take a bribe to pass some faulty buildings some woman from Roanoke built for speculation. That woman was rich and threatened to pull strings to cause Annie's friend to lose her job, but her friend just said, "I been poor before and I may be poor again but I won't pass these houses." And then someone wrote a letter to the editor about the inspector sitting in the courthouse barefoot, when she had just slipped off her shoes a minute on a hot day, and Annie decided to write another letter in her defense.

Annie began to word her letter and Sia realized how painfully all those words came, when they were to be written and scrutinized, how careful and respectful and with what an attempt at dignity, because she knew that her fluid type of conversation would not be suitable for a newspaper. She didn't realize how hard some writers had worked to capture this very fluidity in books and stories she'd never heard of, much less read. Sia wrote down snippets of their conversation in her diary, and descriptions of all of these people and others she saw at the state Fair and at the gas station in town (town being the gas station).

The Rayhill's housekeeper: skimpy gray hair in pink plastic rollers, hunched over with her elbows on her knees, rolling her own cigarettes. Thick body, thin features, she was raised on bread and potatoes, with eyes that look at you through a slight squint as she tells her stories, making sure you're properly impressed. From time to time Robert or the old woman interrupts, then she starts right where she left off without even blinking, very single minded.

"I was born and raised in the country and that's what I like. Used to be all the folk were goin' to the cities, now all the city folks are wantin' to come to the country. I lived with a family once for "bout two weeks right in the middle of Radnor. We had an apartment over the bank. Out the front window was the street and out the back was the parking for the groceries. Wasn't nowhere 't go, just walk up the street and back down it again, go by the shops and window shop. I was busy though. From nine in the morning 'til one the next morning. After I'd get done with the chores and dinner I'd go down't the beauty shop, she had this beauty shop and I'd help in there. Yeah from nine in the morning 'til one..."

The old woman interrupts, "clean ma glasses so's I kin see," and Robert confides that it isn't her glasses, she's got cataracts over her eyes, Dr. says no use to operate now at her age, he says this with the same kind of sage nod he'd use to tell about a freak steer at the state fair.

"...'til one the next morning" (that sage nod again, they all do it, it means you better pay attention and be impressed).

"You worked hard, " Sia said.

"Well you know, you don't work, you don't eat. I stayed there about two weeks and then I went to work at the box factory for awhile."

Then she told how her daughter came and how she went back home and lived for about ten years until her kid was old enough to be left with her grandmother and then she went back to work. She never mentioned a husband and Sia never asked. She'd get out her old plastic billfold and show the pictures of her daughter and son-in-law and the grandchildren.

Sia could never get used to the way Robert and the housekeeper talked about the old lady right in front of her, even though she knew she was supposed to be deaf, she never quite trusted it, those eyes that couldn't see, seemed to hear instead. Whenever it seemed appropriate, or maybe just to interrupt, she'd make some complaint about her condition. "Don't know what's goin' to go wrong with me next, seems like everthin's goin' "wrong."

"Well I guess it should after ninety eight years," Robert would say with just a hint of indignation, "it'll be ninety nine years in November, if she lives that long."

"she says she's got kidney trouble" (the housekeeper now). "Doc says she's clear but she says she ain't, maybe its mental, I hope not, when its mental there's nothin' they kin do. They get old and they get everthin' goin' wrong, or think they do. No, she's bin't the bathroom and says she thinks she's goin' to get all straightened out and then ten minutes later she's in there again complainin' she can't go and she hasn't gone all day, she just don't remember."

The visits to the Rayhills were bleak until one of the widowed daughters came back to live there and help take care of her mother. Lureen was always smiling, always kindly. Robert would tease her for doing laundry on Sunday and then not wanting their neighbors to know. "You wash your face on Sunday doncha?" He'd ask and she'd giggle and tell him he didn't know Helen Baker. Helen Baker wouldn't approve of Lureen doing her laundry on Sunday. And so it went, geriatric problems and gardens and weather and religious philosophy reduced to what one did and didn't do on Sunday.

It was only when Lureen Bagby died, unexpectedly in the hospital of a heart attack after a hernia operation, and only weeks after the 98-year-old mother had finally and quietly expired of simple old age, that Sia realized how much these visits to the "locals" had become an important part of her life.

All those Sunday afternoons she had put on her accent and talked about canning and exchanged ribald jokes in order to draw them out, to make them think she was one of them, to study them, she really had been one of them, she had enjoyed their company as an end in itself. She had learned that among these country folk of limited education and worldly experience there were differences more significant than the difference between their education and hers, the difference was a matter of understanding.

All of them were Christians. There was no question in any of their minds that Jesus was their savior, but there were some who understood the necessity of compassion and tolerance, who understood, one might say, the soul of Christ, and there were those who were not hypocrites only because they did not understand the concept of hypocrisy, who would not do a good deed on Sunday if it involved work.

Sia found among the local population her own friends, people who would reach out to her with a breadth of soul, of understanding that made the differences in their knowledge and experience negligible. She realized that it took a larger understanding to reach out to a newcomer at all, given the reputation of the middle class hippies with their mockery and rejection of the very things in life that had been denied to these long-time country folks, a mockery of their own old desires and disappointments and final resignations. There were few, if any, people from her own cosmopolitan past she would miss as sorely as Lureen Bagby.

Chapter IV

"Another advantage of schizophrenia, perhaps evolutionary, is tirelessness. While a few schizophrenics complain of generalized fatigue, particularly in the early stages of the illness, most patients do not. In fact, they show less fatigue than normal persons and are capable of tremendous feats of endurance... A further thing that schizophrenics do "better' than the rest of us—although it certainly is no advantage in our abstractly complicated world—is simple sensory perception. They are more alert to visual stimuli; as might be expected if we think of them as not having to strain such stimuli through a buffer of consciousness. Indeed, schizophrenics are almost drowning in sensory data. Unable to narratize or conciliate, they see every tree and never the forest. They seem to have a more immediate and absolute involvement with their physical environment, a greater in-the-worldness."

The Origin of Consciousness
in the Breakdown of the
Bicameral Mind.
Julian Jaynes

The fire was very strong and hot. Sia burned the old dry locust saved for the coldest weather. And this locust burned so well that she could throw on a large log of elm or even willow and it would burn, even covered with snow. It was magical, as if the snow were itself a kind of fuel, as if the locust were ever renewable. Around the heater in the front room it was warm enough. The outer edges of the shack were drafty and cold despite rags stuffed around the windows and a quilt hung over the door. You couldn't stay long in a corner without feeling cold.

She had to pile her sleeping bags next to the heater itself with her feet nearly touching it and she knew she'd be up most of the night. She'd fall asleep on one side and wake up later aching on that side but if she turned over she would be cold again and she would be too cold to sleep.

These windy nights seemed eternal. And the dawn would come and she would be totally exhausted and aching, but she would have to go out and work, cut wood in the forest. Once she got up and out, she would be glad. A quarter mile from the shack the wind wasn't as bad and in the forest, the thick screen of trees protected her from it more than the shelter could. Sawing wood kept her warm all through the day.

The wind stopped after two nights and days and the snow fell and then one night there was an ice storm, it was called a "storm" but it was silent at night and in the morning she found the world encased in ice, quiet and beautiful. She walked outside and examined everything, little weeds growing by the creek encased in the thick ice, the little golden stems seemed so deep inside the ice. And all the trees were covered with ice and she could cut no wood until the ice melted and the wood dried a little. She also lacked strength for an ax.

It was too beautiful to be frightening, but she knew her wood supply wouldn't last a week and she would have to find wood down in the forest that she could drag back, twigs and branches, carrying them out would take as much time and effort as cutting larger logs and they would burn so briefly, but still she had to do this and still it kept her warm during the days.

In a few days perhaps there would be a thaw. She was told there were cold spells like this lasting a week or even ten days and some old-timers liked to tell of whole winters like this, no breaks at all. They enjoyed telling these weather horror stories to get attention

She decided that next fall she'd pay someone to put up a proper supply of wood for the winter so she wouldn't have to work so hard and so hopelessly and still be cold. For now, there were still several hours of sunlight in which to work.

Everything she passed, every time she moved, seemed completely ethereal in its coating of ice. She took a child's delight in being in the midst of such beauty, like being part of an intricate sculpture or fantastic painting, it was like living in a painting. As a child she had often wanted so badly, to shrink and become part of something she'd seen in a museum or book, she wanted it so badly and now she was.

In the winter of her twenty-first year, Sia had lain in bed, bed-ridden, sick, despairing. New York City. Lousy jobs, no jobs, stolen car, no place to live, no time for love, no money and lots of bills, medical bills. She lay listening to medieval music at midnight on the radio and the thin rain that fell outside and wind and rain came in through the open window and splashed her legs and she had a dream of country, vast fields of grass and running, almost swimming, through the waving grasses and a girl child playing in a stone courtyard with hair like the grass, in the wind. When she woke up she thought of Calabria in winter and the white and silver tapestry of ice-covered branches, the quietness, all sound stifled by snow. She wrote a poem and it was a prophecy. She wrote her dream but it ended back in the city, in the land of the chained dog, the parked car, the red and blue mail box, all there outside her window: the cruel squalor of the city.

She stayed out all day every day, working and walking and looking at everything. She took all the forest paths, old logging roads, and climbed the mountain in back of her house and down the other side into the town five miles away by the road. It took her all day, stopping to look at everything, all the rocks and trees in their icy metamorphosis. She took a bag of apples and some onion bread. She had picked the apples all fall and stored them in barrels with hay and pieces of torn newspaper and she felt good every time she took one from the barrel.

In town she visited the postmistress who gave her a hot drink and a ride back home before dark. Marie asked her how she was doing and she said fine, hoping that there would soon be a thaw so she could cut wood. Marie invited her to spend the night in town but she declined, sensing that the invite was merely a courtesy and that her actual acceptance would cause discomfort.

The wood was so low and the night so terribly cold she climbed fully clothed into her sleeping bag atop a pile of rugs and quilts with more quilts over top. She thought her tolerance to cold was increased, or perhaps this was a warming trend, and tomorrow she would see the world start to melt and ooze and dry in the sun, for her, for her it would happen, so she could work on wood and prepare for more winter weather. She was warm and sleepy and stayed awake just long enough to appreciate that feeling.

A few hours later she awoke to the ominous sound of the wind and in very little time she was thoroughly chilled. Her body ached with the effort to keep warm. Cold as she was, she was too tired to get up and build a fire and she thought she would wait for morning. Why was this happening again? Again with no break? No time to prepare? She thought that God was battering her, punishing her for her pride, for having what she wanted. No one was to get what they wanted, no matter how simple.

But it wasn't really simple to want beauty, to want to enjoy one's labor, to want no diminishment of one's pride, that went against God or the gods, or whatever, it went against nature. She had to make sacrifices or suffer to make all this right. She shivered and ached through the night, knowing that she would have to work and walk all through the next day to keep warm and that there might not be any real restful sleep until spring, unless she could get some more wood.

She dozed through the nights, waking and turning and shivering and even in her shallow sleep she would freeze and find herself lost and frightened in nightmares that ran like a steady stream beneath her consciousness, just barely beneath, surfacing in frightening memories when she confused nightmares with memory.

The dream city again, She had looked for it all over two continents and throughout her memory and sometimes, riding on a bus through a city, she thought she glimpsed a part of the dream, the serialized nightmare. There are spires in the downtown section and steep hills. The city grows seedy as the hills descend. She is hungry and wants to buy some food. A cafeteria and delicatessen appear. She goes in and eats and the bill is $18. The girl at the counter sees her distress and only charges her half and winks, but that still uses up all her money and now she is destitute. She has nothing. Somehow she must get home. But her home could be a thousand miles away for she doesn't know where she is or how she got there. A drunk is lying on the sidewalk. The people, millions of them all of a sudden, make wide semi-circles around him. Then they all disappear as if lifted up out of the world by celestial wires. He is an Indian. What brought him here? And to this? Perhaps he was always here, before the sidewalks and the buildings and the hundreds of thousands, millions of people. Lying down alone in the wilderness and waking beneath tall grasses, surrounded by mountains, guarded by trees, even in danger, even facing the ferocity of a bear or a mountain lion, even then there is the presence of God, even in fear and death, he is not hopeless. Lying down in the world of green and silence, lying down in one's home and waking on the city street, hundreds of legs and the noise of subways and automobiles and strange buildings, cold concrete and filth in the streams that run in concrete gutters, no trees, no privacy in which to disintegrate, no earth to sink into, no place to hide, and no need, the millions of people turn their heads away from despair and homelessness, they are afraid.

How did she lose her home? Abandonment. It sank into the earth without her, it disappeared. All that is left is this strange dream city where she is always lost and no one recognizes her or knows what she is talking about or cares. She is homeless like the drunk and dying Indian on the street. Perhaps it is his soul in her, a soul fragmented, forgetful of the orderly chronology of reincarnation—life death—the lines of separation blurred. The soul departed a still living body, or just part of it did, leaving behind important knowledge, street names and bus routes—a person could stay lost here forever. Oh no, it is her soul that is leaving, a little at a time, running out like blood in spurts whenever she moves, and she cannot control it.

The girl winks and gives her change, less than a dollar after the tax, perhaps it will do. A bus? It is dark and it is only 4:30, it should have stayed light until 5:00 and she should have seen the sun go down, but she is lost and the sun is hidden by the buildings, and the future and whatever is around the corner, all is hidden from her because she is lost. Next door there are some men in a print shop. It is raining and she takes shelter there and awaits a bus that never comes. They laugh, they say there are no buses anymore. All the people have gone, they get around another way now. She's been gone too long, she doesn't know how they do it, they all just disappeared. There are no buses and the men just laugh. She asks directions but they cannot help her. They just laugh and close up the shop, they have to go home. But she has no home, she has nowhere to go. She doesn't know where she is. They think this is quite a joke but they won't help her. They only laugh and lock and leave. She must wake up, she struggles to wake up and be released. It is another part of the city, each dream She is lost in still another section of the same city and she knows that it is that city, she even recognizes the physical aspects as though she'd been there, in that exact spot before, but she can never move from spot to spot, from dream to dream.

Sia woke up into the hard cold night and thought she should get up and walk outside, up the road, away from the wind. She lay there thinking about that for awhile and then wondered how long she lay there thinking, maybe the night is nearly over and morning will rescue her. She thinks she should get up and check the clock, to know what time it is. It is so very cold now, it must be that hour before dawn when the cold reaches its lowest point, just before dawn. She can't get up to check the time, she can't even turn over to relieve the ache in her side, she has arthritis in that hip now. She is no longer young. She never was. She must get up and build a fire, she is suffering with this cold and she must get warm, but she is too tired to get up and build the fire and she dozes again, perhaps she can dream herself warm. She prays for the morning and dozes reluctantly because she is so very tired.

Sia is afraid to cross the street. It is a rainy night in the city, the neon signs, the headlights of cars all reflected in the rain and forming continuous streaks of eerie light with their own mirror images. Sia stands on the cement island that separated three lanes of cars and trucks going south from three lanes of cars and trucks going north and at the far shore of these respective seas of light and rain and noise and danger were the garish hamburger palaces, beer halls, gas stations and above them the apartment dwellings. These last were the most frightening of all, what horrible sins might be committed in the secrecy of these cramped unlovely cells, tortured children, one reads about them, about so many tortured children. And it is these very children who try to comfort their parents in court, someone told her that. Compassion learned through pain, each child a potential Messiah metamorphosed into a bleeding Christ by the cruelty of the world distilled through one, two people and passed on in concentrated form to the child. This world of neon on combustion engines and all the machines of individual torture and mass destruction, it is hell isn't it? It must be. Even the beautiful quiet forests—even there dwell the people, the would-be gods of ambiguous morality. So Sia was afraid to cross the street and wandered back and forth along the narrow cement island in the rain.

Chapter V

"Our house burned down. We had nowhere to go, so we moved in among the cinders and ruins, just my mother and me. Upstairs a colony of rats had made their home. Their squeaking and screaming terrified me. Mother killed them. Slaughtered them one by one with a long, rusty kitchen knife. She stood on a stool and as they came at her, jumping up, she sundered them from snout to tail or broadside across the body.

"They lay there, purple and rust-like grotesque toys with split seams. She brought the trash can from the yard and laid it on its side and swept them in with a broom she had found with a short blackened handle. The can was heavy, she stood it upright, hugging it against herself and, tilting it slightly, she wheeled it around the yard, circling all over the ground towards the alley. More then her tears or her loneliness, I was hurt by this vision of her in her velvet and lace, wheeling the can of corpses about the yard in this long, unbearable dance. She set fire to them there in the alley and our air was poisoned with the smoke of corpses, wood and carpets."

Sia's journal

Sia worked for other people in the area, gardening, putting up hay, milking, mowing sanding and painting, even baby sitting, anything she could do and someone needed done, and in return they worked for her, cutting logs for her house, helping dig the holes to set the locust posts that would be the foundation of the house, sawing and nailing, building.

She measured the season by the kind of work that was done. The second summer was hot and hard, the time was spent in the woods with chainsaws spitting out sawdust to mingle with the sweat, or kneading sand and mortar and water like dough to just the right consistency, or digging the endless rocks. Some posts couldn't be set as deep as others, some rocks just couldn't be moved, huge tables of rocks that would hold the house up anyway.

The house was to be twenty-feet square with an attic loft. To insure a firm floor, Sia decided to set sixteen foundation posts, each eight feet from the others. It took the entire summer. The autumn was not such a hard time, it was purely beautiful and graceful with the framing of the house with the golden studs sawed at a neighbor's mill from logs cut during the summer. Sia pastured and cared for the man's horses when his own grass was low.

She was lucky in the cooperative spirit of her neighbors. It was slower than money, of course, but it was possible. The money Mary Anne sent covered the mortgage on the land and occasionally there was a little left over for junk food and fuel, not much and not always. Sia learned to walk long distances in all kinds of weather without a thought, or rather, so engrossed in her thoughts that the time, the driving rain or the hot sun, passed over her unnoticed.

By October she needed to buy plywood and roofing paper. She got it on credit at the hardware store/lumber supply yard in the nearest town, thirty miles away over a mountain. She got the house roofed before the first snow and then moved into town where she could walk to work.

She'd gotten herself a job at the hardware store. She shared an old Victorian house owned and rented out by the church with a dozen other young folks who wintered in the town because their shacks were too cold, their houses unfinished, their roads impassable in the heavy snows, or because they couldn't take the isolation.

Sia knew that an entire winter could pass without a single visitor to the lonely hollers. Having survived one such cold and lonely winter, she decided not to do it again until she'd built a real house on the land. She chose this housing arrangement because it was cheap and minimized the time she would have to work to pay for the materials she had already purchased, as well as those she would need to resume work in the spring, but she maintained a remoteness from her housemates.

She was visited several times by different members of the arts co-op, but found herself increasingly detached from them. Each of the other women had connected her life to some cause or effort, rooted herself somewhere. But Sia was more like the ocean; roots were irrelevant to her. She herself was often the connecting force for others, but she was never conscious of this, the same way the river is unconscious, careless of its passengers. But while the dangers of the river are well known, the dangers of rootless people are only understood after it is too late.

Once a week, on a Saturday afternoon, she treated herself extravagantly to a milkshake in the town's drugstore. She sat for exactly ninety minutes (a milkshake hardly entitled her to more time on a stool) and listened to the girls at the fountain talking to each other, to other young women who wandered in and out with babies on their ample hips, to the young men who teased them elaborately and even to the old men with their mild hopeless lechery. She dressed not in her usual jeans, but in a skirt she had bought at the Dollar store down the street. Thus disguised, she was able to witness everything without them being aware of her interest.

Everything was a joke to these people, nothing was stated outright, not even complaints about the government, the weather, the illnesses and intractability of children, or having to work so hard and still not being able to make it. These small town folks were satirists, albeit of an unsophisticated variety. Sia could guess at the severity of their troubles, but though they might take to drink in response, they never complained, except by making a joke of it. Every misfortune was fair game for humor—it had to be that way.

Her other pleasure was a more private kind, only one person knew of it. Whenever she felt in the mood and had the time, she borrowed the firehouse key from the post mistress (a sympathetic lady with infinite tolerance) and went upstairs to the dance hall where they held the fund raising dances, the fourth of July celebrations, and the baby showers. There she played Bach, Scarlatti and Couperin on the deplorable old upright.

As she played, Sia planned her house, dreamed her home. The music became her home. Softly played, the music became the black velvet night, mist-like against her skin—she could feel it. It was rain on leaded glass and wind in the trees, mirrors reflecting night or dawn, stars and snow and rocks. All of her homes merged into this music, her childhood home, her dream home, her home of stone.

A dream, living through fire everywhere, and then the freezing stones against the glass, the hail of music against the window and the harsh, salty, stone-like snow beating against the window. Stones, she dreamt of them. Stone paths and stone walls, a stone house, a stone gazebo in a garden, red Japanese maples, white dogwoods and blue spruce and lilacs everywhere around the stone gazebo and a garden path pink with pink stones and green and smooth with the oval flat stones like jades in every imaginable shade of green and black shining and crystal white sharp, walking barefoot over the rough massage of the myriad stones and over the cool smoothness of large gray slabs, climbing a green and golden hillside studded with stones that throb with multi-colored veins. stones, rocks, boulders as large as small houses, covered with vines, hiding dead leaves in crevices, guarding the secret entrances to the earth. Stones molded and sculpted by water that comes up violently in the night in May and dries up in June. Stones that hold up the ancient oversized trunks of leaning trees caught in mid-fall by the boulders, boulders split by the roots of trees, stones covered with thorns and stones that shelter.

Sia missed her house like a lover. She would play her dream stone home, accelerating until she played too fast, struggling to keep up with the music, then abruptly stop, tired, and go back to her rented room to sleep another night in exile.

She would remember music through the night, how her mother had played the piano until dawn, molding images and dreams that Sia would never forget. Sia had never seen her mother sleep. Whenever she heard the Mozart Sonata in A major she drifted back into infancy, listening to her mother practice the same two measures of sixteenth notes endlessly through the night, and she remembered remembering strong hands, molding, carving, shaping, stroking stone.

When weather and finances permitted, Sia drove over the mountain to the half-finished house. On weekends she stock-piled mortar mix from the hardware store and large flat rocks from her own creek and when the piles of rocks provided her with sufficient variety and quantity, she began to rock face the plywood sides of the house.

She started the first rocks right on the ground, confident that the West Virginia bedrock soil would hold the weight. Here and there she hammered nails into the mortar, these nails were placed to hold the stones while she applied the mortar around them. She learned from experience the right consistency of the mortar for this work. It couldn't be as wet as the mortar they had poured into the holes around the foundation posts, but she couldn't work with it if it was too dry.

She worked with a trowel and with her fingers as well, even though the mortar made her hands dry and uncomfortable. She couldn't manipulate the stuff as well with just the trowel, and she found that when she used her hands to smooth and push the mortar around the stones if felt like a kind of sculpture to her, and she thought that someday she would like to learn to sculpt, to model, but mostly to carve.

She dreamed about carving with tiny tools, using a supreme patience to wear away the wood or the stone perfectly and smoothly into the forms she chose, with textures of skin and velvets and furs and feathers. It would take very small tools and infinite patience. She dreamed it often, and with the patience growing in her as she slowly built up the rock, she was content that some day she would indeed do this.

The rock work progressed extremely slowly. Many weekends she was snowed out of the valley or didn't have money for gas. Whenever she did manage to get there, she began by running her hands over the rough, multi-colored and multi-textured surface of the work she had already completed.

Then she would mix her mortar in the deep wheelbarrow and begin to stretch the rock upward. The rocks she worked with were the worn-down pieces of boulders that had once been the base of mountains—the creeks had worn the very mountains down. She could still find boulders on the hillsides as large or larger than the house. These boulders were conglomerations of quartz, feldspar, mica and silica, shaped and amalgamated by the pressure of glacial floods and then worn and refined by water to an infinite variety of shapes. She also found, in the creeks, limestone that the water had melded with the skeletons of shellfish and small animals, pressured and heated to a mineral state, and glistening siliceous sandstone reddened with iron oxide and calcite and clay, but these fell apart and were not suitable to work with.

Back in town, after work, Sia would walk down the street to the library and order books from bibliographies of other books she'd ordered. The librarian sent all over the country for books for Sia, books on stone carving and wood carving and geology and history, as well as novels by Faulkner and Flannery O' Conner and Eudora Welty and Carson McCullers. They talked often of literature and it always amazed Sia that the prim lady-like librarian read one murder mystery every night and Sia borrowed these too, reading took her mind off things.

With the reading and the stone work, the winter passed quickly. Spring brought floods, washed out roads that had been snowed in anyway all winter, and left them rutted, rocky and impassable for the summer. Sia quit her job and returned to the house to stay.

Sia was so immersed in her reading and the construction of the house that she didn't notice when Mary Anne missed a monthly payment. When the bank notified her, she was unable to contact Mary Anne for several weeks and she had to keep making excuses to the banker. When she finally reached Mary Anne from the pay phone at the gas station, she was so distraught that she caught herself screaming, and she was embarrassed to think she'd been heard during the Sunday service going on in the little church across the road. Mary Anne told her to relax, it would all work out for the best, things always did, but it wasn't precisely a promise.

Finally, the holder of their deed of trust arranged the sale of the property, the proceeds to pay off the debt to the bank and what was left to go to Mary Anne and Sia. Sia continued to soothe her spirit working on the stone, but by the day before the sale, the house was still primarily exposed wood, exquisite and vulnerable.

Sia always enjoyed the dawn of early spring days. She'd get up when it was still dark and build and bank the fire as she watched the pale pink in the eastern sky, then she'd walk a mile or so up the road watching the morning mist lift from the mountains. Usually she would stop awhile to contemplate her progress on the house, which had become like a living organic being. That last morning in West Virginia, she took with her a can of kerosene and some matches and some kindling, just to be sure.

She thought about Pompeii and bodies buried by volcanic ash. She remembered a book that a friend had given her on the origin of the planet, written by a woman who was a poet-geologist. In this book was described the formation of the petrified forest of Arizona, which Sia now longed to see. The Petrified Forest had once been a large forest of fir trees that were felled and buried by flooding, muddy streams. The mud had protected the trunks from oxygen and decay. Then volcanic eruptions covered them over with another shroud of ash, preserving them for the millions of years required for the wood tissue to be replaced, cell by cell, with mineral crystals of blood-red, translucent green, pale blue, white, purple and brown. Where there had been cracks in the tree trunks, places where fungi and lichens could have grown, there now grew clusters of amethyst and clear quartz.

The author speculated upon the image of the human corpses of Pompeii, embalmed in volcanic ash, being metamorphosed into semi-precious stones, if only they had been left to lie undisturbed through the eons, like the fir trees of the Petrified Forest. Sia found this image far superior to that of the shriveled mummies of ancient Egypt, a "form more suitable" she wrote "to eternity." She pondered why human kind had such trouble understanding eternity, couldn't quite grasp it, even though they were as entitled to its peace as the trees and the rocks.

She sat for hours by the edge of the creek that morning, mesmerized by the patience of the water, its soothing sound as it worked on the earth; it seemed so purposeful to her. Human beings lived so hastily, running helter-skelter, making mistakes, destroying what they built, and then they had to keep coming back to start over, working each time with different pieces of the same puzzle, never seeing the whole. She thought she would have liked, at that moment, for her soul to permeate the stones in the creek and work there patiently, creating slowly the inevitable perfection of crystals of color and light. She wished to become petrified and protected from the frightening free-fall of human life.

Her internal thoughts became a conversation, consciousness divided.

"I am having a dialogue with my self, and I never did really have dialogues with the others, all of those folks. I just drew them out to observe them, like specimens, like the rocks and water and trees, specimens. They are specimens of gods' work and I was looking for God."

"That's embarrassing, gods' work."

"But it's true. I was only interested in nature and in art, I wanted to be God too, and create perfect works. I was looking to find God in me."

"Some people think that's evil, they call it the inspiration of the devil."

"Maybe they're right. Certainly to me, it is only human life and progress that makes no sense, the rest is pure beauty, and all things working out for the terrible and catastrophic best. Maybe there is that division between God and the devil, and maybe the god-in-us is really the work of the devil trapping and twisting divine inspiration and energy to evil ends. I don't know. I don't know. How patient we can be when we know what we're doing, how hurried and anxious when we don't Now I am rushing again because I don't know where to go."

Sia knew it was wrong to burn the house and the surrounding trees, driving out the deer and small animals that wandered near it. But she knew she'd be plagued forever if she didn't. She felt like she was protecting a child from rape. She had to make a choice. She made it only once, then let one step lead to her next.

First, she built a pile of kindling just as for a campfire, in the middle of the house. She poured the kerosene in rivulets from the kindling out to the four corners of the house. The lumber had been green when first cut, but had aged uncovered for three seasons of the year, and it was a clear, dry day with a bit of breeze from the creek. She lit the fire and watched the sudden eruption of flame, and then walked out the door, leaving it wide open behind her. She had opened all the windows of the house before building the fire. She went back down to the creek and watched her work disappear in flames and chaos.

Blood-red flames peeled back the containing skin, and the flame-red blood flowed free in the air, bubbles transparent. Sia saw the studs burn and collapse, the tar paper melt, the metal insulation backing reflect the red flames, the blood of the house. She imagined the bloody arms of women holding up the roof, stretching it to the flame-red sky before it collapsed. She remembered the windows of her house as she would walk back to it from the woods at sunset, the sinking sun, the windows suffused with the glow of sun fire burning inconceivable millions of miles away, "light years" away, the single composite word "light year" bespeaking a terrible philosophical twist, consigning time and space back to chaos, back to the purity of dreams untouched by the myriad flaws of reality.

Chapter VI

In the dream
bloodless rootless
I wandered through a fiery day
created once in reality for me
but not rooted in time
not experienced with blood.

When the house was gone, but for a square of stones and piles of charred debris and burned trees, the sky clouded over and spilled rain down on the scene, putting out the fire and washing the coal-black trunks of the trees, making them shiny in the gray dusk. Soon the rain turned to snow; the last spring storm was underway.

By the time Sia walked back down the creek bed to the road, it was covered with snow, and the wind raged at her as it did every spring, making a final statement, like that last burst of cold before the dawn. Sia had no thought to wait until the storm abated, but started out immediately in the truck, headed for Roanoke, then Washington, D.C. and finally New York City. There was enough gas, change and music to get her to Mary Anne's apartment, and beyond that she didn't think.

She put a tape in the player—Scarlatti on one side, Couperin on the other. The music articulated the landscape. Hard edged music, it defined the shale and granite and limestone and angled branches beneath the softening and numbing snow, the buried land she was leaving behind. Stately, it labored slowly up the steep rocky hills. In cascading, brittle arpeggios, it shaped the waterfalls, the frothing, bubbling pools, and all the shapes that water took over rocks, and all the shapes and textures, slab-like and hollow, rough and sharp and stippled, that rocks took under water, the large boulders embraced by vines and dead branches that looked like one thing or another in the various shadings of the seasons. Scarlatti pricked her visual memory and rushed past her like the highway signs at fifty, sixty, seventy miles per hour.

The tape ran out in the middle of a piece and she turned it over to the dead winter of Couperin: white branches through the white fog over the river, shadows of boats on the river, shadows of weeds and trees, so white and misty; images like the paintings in a museum following one another in a stately, gloomy procession. Then there was a cheerful piece that woke her up. Then she played another tape of Bach Inventions and remembered playing them on the piano, her fingers working independently of her mind, the mystery and the beauty of it, she had buried herself in it, all those years before in the cities. She sank into the music, sinking into the garden soil, sinking into visions, dying, dying.

"I have lived all my life in a room—white walls, a bed, a dresser, a chair and an open window. Outside I can see a single tree and the gray T. V. screen through the window in a distant house. Someone brings a tray of food and leaves. The events of my life are the cold wind on my legs when I've kicked the covers off; the brief, quiet rain at night when everyone else is asleep; the movement of the branches outside my window. A caterpillar crawls and grows to dragon dimensions. I see my life as though under water or through undulations of heat. I take my face to the window and we look out at the rain, and when my face is at the window people passing know that this is a house of insanity.

All the sensations of memory and dream conspire to reveal and elude. Shadows and parts of shadows. I sleep. I feel pain. I cry, but only I can hear, though everyone watches me. I feel them. I dare not look. I hear, put two and two together, and remember. My mother's face looking at something else. Who knows I am here? The music is so low that only I can hear it—in the dark of my room—and their footsteps outside, walking back and forth over the soft carpet. The crack of floorboards—the sound is buried deep. I lie here talking and crying, all these things, all these things. I think my mother is listening at the door in the darkness, but I hear the footsteps back and forth across the house. There is carelessness in the sound. I strain to hear the urgencies and the angers, the sorrows in the footsteps and the whispers outside my door. I hear everything and know the violence and the tragedies, and in the daytime I tread a careful life.

My mother is a bird. My mother is a shell that I cannot get into. I look into windows of basement apartments and I see laundry baskets and beds of poverty, heavy dressers with mirrors, a pink and blue page on a stucco wall. It frightens me to remember the house. Whose? Where? My mother does not know. I do not ask her.

To be in the water and see myself through the water in me, like a beautiful transparent fish. To see the water in and out of me, and to flow with the current and allow the current to flow through me. To be in the water and to be the water.

My self yearns to be one with the water and with the fire that holds my eyes, at one with the room and all my terrors and all my sorrows.

I seem to surround, with my fluid body, and be surrounded by a kind of roving pillow. Together we were all movement and nebulous form. I had this dream many times when I was three or four. I suppose I was remembering my birth. I don't remember birth now, but I remember the dream of remembering. I also dreamed of a world deserted. I went out on the block and looked down the street and there was no one, and I went back into the house and sat on the floor and waited. I had no fear. I saw in my mind, in my dream, the street extending out to the entire world, one long, dusty street.

I must have been remembering some knowledge learned before birth. I don't remember life before the birth, but I remember the dreams. They are the only guide I have. But that cannot be, for at birth the ego has grown to a size large in the womb, and in my dream the ego is minuscule. I must have still been a seed in my mother's womb, feeling the gentle commotion, the man and woman making love, the tender, vehement vibrations of the woman's orgasm.

"Driving down Atlantic Avenue between mounds of snow from the last spring storm, looking up the side streets, dilapidated shacks and tenements interspersed with enormous stone public buildings modeled after Florentine palaces, Moorish palaces, Georgian palaces, a World War I monument, pillars roofed and massive framing, the snow beach, the ocean, desecrated daily, the sand washing up black and oily, a desolate pier. Further south, mansions built with the ostentation and exuberance of the twenties, crowding and cheapening each other on too little land. Houses turn seedy again, churches advertising Bingo, names on businesses, all bespeak the age and decay of folks who never went anywhere, who watched the world change as the overwhelming human floods visited every summer.

"And the opulence again, driving into Ventnor City. Row after row of mausoleums commemorating other eras. Some people walked carrying groceries, looking cold, disinterested, and totally unaware of the historical, even archaeological fascination their city held. Later, two figures standing in the cemetery along the highway turned out to be statues. All the living people were warm and private behind their venetian blinds.

"Taverns, diners, motels advertising pools and TV, factory outlets and warehouses, then scrub oak and pine, burnt-out house frames, backyard gas stations and 'antique' shops, chicken runs, cabins for rent, all in a row on the highway, all kinds of supplies, beer, and then the scrub oak and pine give way to cattails, swamps, and later to the flat, vast truck gardens.

A man, well wrapped in multi-colored rags, works on a broken-down bus that slumps beside the demolished hulls of two other buses. Various parts lay about the ground, and a fire flares from a large tin can where he goes often to warm his hands.

"More towns. Tractor sales, Disco dancing, one-room shacks, larger houses with many mailboxes, rooming houses, a door left open on a 20 degree day; scenes of trysts, murders, grinding poverty, cunning and despair, and the loss of love or honesty, what sort of person could survive such rooms, those walls? Some neat, tidy houses of the thirties and forties, yellow or pink "stucco" with cactus plants on ledges under arches, they look like old ladies, widowed for decades, lonely and cheerful and doggedly Christian.

"Some new houses, outlandish additions to frame houses or venetian-blinded brick "ranchers" look like young women, tolerant of husbands and kids, reducing, making up, hair-curling, nail polishing, saving up for a French Provincial bedroom suite from Sears, plastic flowers, vinyl slipcovers, and after the bedroom suite, a fancy mirror, a larger freezer, looking forward to cheerful widowhood and dogged Christianity.

"Viewed from a thousand years hence, we could not truly know what lives these structures sheltered, could not even guess at the innermost striations of illusions and sorrows that went unrecognized, so skillfully hidden were they beneath the siding, the 2x4's, the sheetrock, the skin and sinew and bone.

"A house, very old, at least a century, seen from the road across a field, a stream and a second field. It is in Delaware, on the road to New Jersey. I have seen it countless times. I will never see who lives in it or know if anyone lives in it.

"Driving along Atlantic Avenue, looking up the streets of houses of every kind of architecture. I had the premonition that tonight I would dream again of being lost in the infinite, unknowable city. Lila once told me about a man who came into her office drunk, to get a refund. She told him to come back when he was sober, because he had to fill out forms. He passed out while she was telling him this and she called an ambulance, and they called the police to take him to the drunk tank.

"Later he came back, sober, very charming, she said, to get his refund. She asked him if he remembered passing out in front of her? No. Did he remember the police taking him? No. All he remembered was waking up in jail. She asked him why he drank, she told him he was such a nice man. When he was leaving, she asked if he was going out to buy a drink, and he said, 'No, you were nice to me today, I don't think I'll drink today.' The other people in the office were shocked. How could she talk like that to a man like that? They were afraid of his drunkenness. They didn't want to know about his problem, they didn't want to see him.

"I have often felt in my dream that I am doomed to being eternally lost because no one will help me, because no one will listen to try to understand that I am misplaced, because ultimately no one will so much as recognize me. They look past or through me and annihilate me. In all existence, I am completely lost. Writing about it now, I make it sound like a philosophical observation on the modern alienation of human beings from one another. But in my dream, my recurring nightmare, it is terrifying in a physical way, like drowning. And truly I am dying."

Sia's journal

Wild rooster in the barn,
dog killed it,
it cried like a child.
Far away
screams of terror
and pain,
then quiet,
bloody, slow dying.
Deer in the forest,
strange sounds of fear in the night,
the doe's skull bleached white,
killed by bears,
shot by men in passing cars,
eaten by flies,
birds,
stray dogs.
Cow dung,
rat shit,
wood burning,
damp wood rotting,
wet dogs
and apple wine
and onions cooking,

smell
the sea air,
faint after so many miles

I am gray
and slightly damp
and old like the woods
and alone.

I waited nights,
watched the headlights
on the ceiling move
past the window
up the road,
waited to hear a car door slam,
answered questions of strangers at my door,
waited,
and watched the moon,
alone.

I listen to birds,
so many different kinds,
and the shrieks of chickens,
like a distant human chorus,
like the singing of the dead.

I hear songs
and dream of sirens.
I am an ancient sybil,
resurrected in all my anguish.

I walk up the road at night,
I get out of the way of cars,
I wait.

The mountains move in
closer on me,
I do not sleep.
I wait.

I go to the cave
to look at the river,
I look at the sky,
I go home
and sit in my chair,
drink wine,
listen,
and wait
for the dawn.

The gas range is creamy yellow
with a hinged black top,
salvaged from a demolished house in town,
antique.
I turn to cook trout
and think I am not here.

I am lakes in granite caverns
and moss that shrouds the stone.

They will eat the fish
and use the stove,
bathe,
do laundry,
right here in the kitchen,
this kitchen.
I am not here
I am on the bus,
cold,
sleepy,

no place to go,
to stretch,
to sleep.

East coast to west coast,
I stop at each town,
look it over,
consider
starting a new act.

There are towns in Pennsylvania
full of gas stations
and railroad tracks
and gray frame houses,
with porches
and wicker rockers
and nothing else,
nothing there.

Greasy restaurants,
old candy bars,
old gray men,
looking,
looking.
They are watching the mists
roll down the mountains,
standing on the porch
together.

I ride across the continent
from town
to town
to empty town.
I get lost,
I cry,

I am alone,
and people stare
at my grief,
my glamour,
my memories.

Bus station bathrooms,
hot water in rusty basins,
mirrors in yellow light,
I turn on the faucet,
it hurts my wrists,
so cold under the hot water,
my blood,
my heart,
remembering
the fish
stuck in my throat.
I gave it to the cat.
I bend
to give the fish to the cat,
and straighten,
and moving,
remember
each movement as a memory
gleaned from an eternity.

I wash the dishes,
go to bed.
I am not there.
I hear so many voices
and see no one,
childrens' voices mostly.

I dream of Italy,
colored strips of plastic

blowing in doorways,
and mournful music,
and marble floors.
I hear footsteps on hot gravel,
black lace and marble,
clothes lines.
I will never see Italy again.

They eat the fish.
They are still now,
happy.
They talk about cows, bees,
a new chicken house.

My mind us spherical,
like the evening mist.
I am a ghost
and on one sees me.
I listen to the footsteps,
as though on marble,
and walk the road at night.
I see my face in the window
and don't recognize it immediately.
I am not here.
I am not here.
I am alone,
in bus stations,
in lonely slumbers,
in history,
a hermitess walking the road

Sia's journal

Chapter VII

In the cathedral
rootless of Christ
bloodless of martyrs
I hold the art
of the plucked dead flower in my hand
rooted in stone
in earth
and see the brown blossom
alive
with the livingness of change.

Sia's truck broke down North of Roanoke and she almost froze sleeping out the night in the cab. By morning it warmed up considerably and she hitched a ride with a van full of folks heading for New York City. As a passenger she soaked in the scenes that passed by the window through the countless miles back to New York.

Sia noted that in New York people had "places," everyone had to have a place to be at a given time. But not "homes." "Home" implies permanence, comfort, uniqueness, a place that takes on the personality of the owner. Sia knew people who had lived in an apartment for twenty years, but could not call it a home. The permanence was an accident, sometimes a tragedy.

She passed a vacant lot where someone had planted sunflowers a year earlier and they still towered brown above the tangle of broken, weedy tomato plants and the ghostly cornstalks and the litter of creeping squash vines. There were such gardens planted here and there in vacant lots of the city, among the broken bottles and scattered trash. Sia thought of them as coded messages passed on by people who didn't always understand, but who were plagued with some inexplicable yearning that could be satisfied no other way. The message was ignored by most people, who allowed their yearning to become a quiet, subtle anger, making them old and eventually killing them.

How did this happen? Why did we abandon nature, our original home, for this alienation? Once built, this city, like some kind of chemical waste, could not be disposed of; it would not decompose slowly and elegantly back into the natural cycle, not without some terrible cataclysmic destruction taking with it, all the warm-blooded things, dying to feed a new geologic future and god knows what else.

Of course Sia was crazed to even imagine this. Most people were satisfied with the city, considered its lifestyle superior in every way to everything else everywhere else. To Sia, New Yorkers, with all their resources to enjoy the cultural life of the city, were the most provincial people she had yet to come across. To her, the deliberately windowless buildings were a desecration. How could one look at a painting by Van Gogh without smelling the fresh air? Or listen to music without the undercurrent of wind in the trees? Dancing was something everyone should do after a day of harvest. One should live with harvesting and dancing and music and the surrounding visions of beauty unconfined by the ninety-degree angles of a canvas.

Sia had lived in strange big cities most of her life, but there was nothing so terrifying as New York City with no place to go. She panicked. She had Mary Anne's new address and she knew exactly where it was, but she wasn't ready for Mary Anne yet.

She rode the subway aimlessly until it emerged into daylight and rumbled on its elevated track past the intimate hidden backsides of desperate lives. She passed broken windows patched with plastic and newspaper, laundry hung hopelessly to dry in the soot, always on rickety back porches, tiny little porches arranged like tiny squares drawn uncertainly on a piece of scratch paper. Some people locked their bicycle to the railing of the porch; other people had plants half dying, half surviving on the porch; and still others had a washing machine with its cord trailing back inside the kitchen; but most people had damp and gray laundry, all looking alike, sheets and undershirts getting moldy in the summer damp or frozen board-like in the deceptive early spring sun.

Sia saw a child sitting at a table covered with blue and white oil cloth and playing with jars, but the train sped by too quickly for her to see what he was doing. She kept trying to see into the apartments, to see into the lives, but the train sped by. She could see down the streets, between the windows, that the fronts of the apartment buildings looked cleaner and safer and nicer than the sides that faced the train. Everything broken or dirty was shoved to the back.

As she sped through the Bronx toward the suburbs, everything became cleaner and safer and nicer. She got off at the last station amid the flying debris of old newspapers and candy wrappers and waited for the return train to Mary Anne's place.

Mary Anne had a small room behind the kitchen with a cot that Sia appropriated. Mary Anne seemed relieved she didn't want one of the bigger rooms. The apartment was on the lower east side, on the second floor of a large ornate stone building with iron gates over the door, sandwiched between a laundry and a once elegant Chinese restaurant. The entire neighborhood was due for renovation, but in the meantime it was available to Mary Anne and her friends.

Sia conned her way into a secretarial job despite her unskilled approach to a typewriter and her total ignorance of shorthand, primarily because the office was in a museum in which antiquities were stored, catalogued and occasionally displayed, and she still had some knowledge of Greek and Latin. She was also able to summarize correspondence sent in French and German, although she couldn't draft responses that were very sensible.

When it was her turn to take the minutes of the curators' monthly meetings, she scribbled sketches of the pompous participants and used her extraordinary memory to satirize the proceedings with an uncanny ear for the idiosyncratic patterns of speech of the various individuals. Her boss laughed at them and thoroughly enjoyed them, then asked her to please reconstruct something that he could turn in at the next meeting. She was poorly paid but felt secure she wouldn't be fired. What she enjoyed about the job was the walk through its darkened rooms at the end of the day, but once outside, she realized she had completely missed the sun and this depressed her immensely.

Also depressing were the shops near the museum full of everything expensive, whether food or furniture. There was never anything whatsoever she could afford, not that she would have wanted any of it were it not thrust under her nose. She would walk into the stores on her walk to the bus or the subway to escape the cold evening air for awhile. Even when it began to get downright balmy she was always cold and sometimes wore two shirts at a time under her sweaters. The ride home took forever and she couldn't get a seat for most of it. On the subways she watched the people, one woman well on her hormonal way to being a man, who seemed to be retarded as well. She was always on the train, as if she lived there, but of course to some other observer it could be said that Sia was always on the train too. The most disturbing thing about this strange ugly woman on the train was that Sia thought she had seen her once before in an apartment window overlooking Sia's bus route, leaning out the window and watching the traffic, but also at the same time masturbating, and such obliviousness to her embarrassing lack of privacy upset Sia terribly. So she watched the strange woman's face trying to determine if she was the same woman from the window. She thought she must be because she was also totally oblivious to Sia staring at her. And she did get off at a stop near the apartment building Sia remembered as the site of her traumatic vision.

One night she dreamed of the wood workers she had met in West Virginia, and she met their urban counterpart the next day. He was a maker of harpsichords and clavichords and had transformed his Riverside Drive apartment into a medieval-esque workshop, the walls covered with pencil sketches of the animals and faces he carved on his elaborate music stands. He had a supply of all kinds of woods: cherry, walnut, ebony, and hundreds of candles, lest the electricity go out on him, as he preferred to work at night and never forgot the blackout of 1965.

When Sia visited him the candles cast shadows that flicked and danced with the rhythms of their speech and this fascinated and frightened her. He told her intimate details of his past lives and she was glad he wasn't one of those who vividly remembered being Napoleon or Ramses III. He had just been ordinary anonymous people. She liked the way he took for granted that she would believe him, that he didn't have to explain or defend his perfectly logical belief in reincarnation, but just got down to the juicy details. He was just as unabashed in discussing his homosexuality, and Sia enjoyed his candor and wit. Unfortunately, she never saw him again, as he up and left for Mexico the next day. She never did find out what happened to the workshop.

Sia was extraordinarily lonely and wandered around the streets in the late summer nights, forgetting where she lived. Sometimes when she went to work in the mornings she couldn't remember how old she was, where she was, what part of her lengthening life was waiting for her on the other side of her dreams. She was never quite sure if it would be her mother or someone else standing in the kitchen, and Mary Anne asked her if she was alright with a suspicious look on her face. Sia stopped talking to anyone and spent her weekends at the Cloisters where the music soothed her.

She grew so tired and lethargic that she quit her job and spent entire weeks at the Cloisters just sitting, and Mary Anne felt too guilty about the house in the woods to demand any rent. She tried to remember things. She tried to remember her truck that had broken down in Virginia, the night she slept in the cab of it listening to the rain and dreaming of drowning, but not really, not painfully. She tried to recall the group that picked her up, their travels together, meandering around the east coast, dropping off people and picking up new ones. She couldn't remember any of their names now. She remembered the fire most vividly, but couldn't remember the house at all, which was most terrifying because she had worked on it such a long time, with such care. She remembered the process but couldn't visualize the result.

Every day Mary Anne would say, "Are you alright?" and cock her head a little while Sia answered "Yes I'm okay" and then Mary Anne would wrinkle her eyes up like she knew something Sia didn't know she and say "Well, if you say so" and shrug and go her way.

Then Sia would touch things, usually something made of wood, as if she felt she were being blown away by a huge wind and needed to grab onto something to anchor herself.

Surrounded by windows
reflecting walls
isolated
watch circularly
cloud-ward
windowed eyes
arrange leaves and debris
in multiple perceptions
lights
vibrations
whispered laughter
whispered anger
whispers
insane and many
crawling walls
joy down
deathward
leave
through crevices of brick

and stone
silent in the noisy dawn
begging with eyes
on streets.
Travel far
from the warmth of cells
kitchen cots
empty anonymous mornings
to the ends of trains
duck beneath the shadows of birds
black asphalt crawling
upside down heads laughing
from windowed eyes
stoned crevices
disconnected
Coney Island Carnival music
and the dirge of the river below
the bridge
beneath watchful eyes
mercury tears grow around her
like an egg
a magic egg
she is a magician
afraid and delighted
she turns percussive blood
into music playing drunk in a storm
southern rain remembered
strange dissonance
that caught the heart of a witch
and she loved her dangerously
she remembers and berates an old
guitar materialized out of her instant
desire and then she collapses
savoring weakness

and he caresses her
and she drams she lay with the
bear in the mountain.

Sia's Journal

For several weeks Sia slept. She was afraid to go outside where the lights and noises assaulted her. She was rarely hungry, and when she was she ate whatever she found in the refrigerator without noticing what she was eating. She wrote some poetry whenever she awoke, rather mechanically, as if to note down a dream, as if instructed to do so. She'd sleep, wake, write a poem, eat some rice or bread, sit staring at the kitchen window or at the blackened wall on the other side of the room, until her eyelids sank and her spine sank, then she'd sleep again.

Mary Anne thought she was ill and should see a doctor, but Sia thought she was dying and wanted to be left alone. Mary Anne was glad the day Sia decided to go out to the Cloisters, but she was puzzled when Sia handed her a pile of papers without a word. Mary Anne saw they were poems and put them some place to read later, when she had more time and nothing else to do. Mary Anne had never been into poetry.

When Sia left the Cloisters it was dark, not the peaceful, star-broken dark of the mountains, but the furtive gray dark of the city, hiding the hectic fears and anxieties of the night. She hated this five o'clock twilight, this ambiguity. People were walking briskly to their cars or to bus stops to wait for buses that they seemed to feel sure would come. Some people walked briskly to holes in the ground to find their subway trains. Everyone walked briskly, knowing where they were going, not aware enough to be frightened by the deadlines of that half dark.

Sia did not know where she could go now. She dreaded going back to the apartment that was always crowded with Mary Anne and her friends. Even without her friends, Mary Anne crowded the apartment with her chatter, her messiness, her absurdity. Sia couldn't go back there now, feeling as fragile as she did. Fragile, frightened, as if she expected a blow from above to shatter her completely, physically, mentally, emotionally, what other ways could she be shattered? Whatever ways there were, she felt she would be shattered in every way if she went back just now to the noise and the close heat and the cooking odors.

It was life she wished to avoid just now, or at least the evidence of life lived badly.

She kept walking as she thought, walking quickly and with a semblance of purpose, even though she didn't know where she was going. Someone fell in beside her, was talking to her. At first his voice blended in with the voices overheard around her. This man was lecturing her, telling her not to look so sad, that she shouldn't be alone. But his concern for her was not kind or sincere. His concern was menacing in what it implied.

She kept on walking, trying to ignore the reality of this new voice, but he kept on walking beside her and talking to her, and as he edged closer to her she was forced to turn in the directions he wished her to take. He was directing her to walk where he wanted her to go.

He was poor and shabby. He could be young, but he was weathered and beaten. He appeared old, but his voice was young and his remarks were stupid.

This kind of thing happened from time to time. It was annoying but not usually frightening. She could freeze these strange men out in a matter of minutes. But this man was not usual. He was menacing in his stupidity. He was smoking and looking sideways at her as he talked to see her reaction. He almost looked shrewd when he glanced at her that way, but the banality of his talk defeated his posing. His accent was rural, of the mountains. He might have hitched a ride to the city just today. Yesterday he might have been burning barns or fucking cows, that's how she pictured the vague person behind the ignorant, insulting voice.

They had reached a dead end to the path, a wall overlooking the river. He leaned against the wall, smoking his cigarette, and she turned as if to go, but he caught her arm with his free hand and said "Don't go yet." Although his body was relaxed and he still faced away from her toward the river, his grip on her arm was very firm, very insistent, and his voice had changed when he told her not to go, there was no plea in this, it was pure command.

She began to be afraid, even realizing that at this point it was fear more than anything else that could hold her here against her will. There was still time to struggle, to run, if she dared. But the night was dark and she didn't know where she was going, she didn't know where she would run to or who she could call. She turned and leaned against the wall beside him and he let go of her arm and continued to talk. He talked a long time, she didn't listen. Once she thought he started to cry, but it was over before she could shift her attention from the fantasies that occupied her.

In self defense she withdrew so far within herself that she felt herself expand into several women, all confined together within the bones of her one single body. It was extraordinary, this feeling of fragmentation, as if something inside a tight wrapping had shattered. It was as if her eyes had revolved inward to watch secret scenes inside herself, and the first was a procession of all her selves hooded and caped as if in a medieval ritual. The music of the Cloisters reverberated in her head and the selves she watched moved slowly to that rhythm. They moved closer and expanded to become the background for more scenes, and as the scenes grew larger and closer the music faded farther and farther and then disappeared, so that everything happened in silence, faces screamed at her in utter silence.

Some people walked through the park with a dog and she was reminded of a bear in the mountains, but this vision was outside herself and vague, whereas the visions that emerged within were clear and vividly detailed. She saw men ploughing a field, the same ones she had seen in an old dream. She noticed the thickness and color of their clothing and their gnarled, begrimed hands. She noticed the clods of black earth and could imagine its feel, and she felt as if she herself were being churned up and ploughed into this earth. Coming up to the surface of it and reaching for the sky, for breath, and being stirred back down to the bottom of it, the earth and her body churning and twisting as if it were the sea and she were drowning, drowning in the black earth of grain fields.

The man's voice took on the distant droning quality of a chant, a dirge, the procession of hooded men, or women, she didn't know, walking in measured steps and chanting this dirge for her. As they came closer his voice rose and quickened, and she realized with a small fragment of her mind that he was growing angry.

She wondered if she knew him, owed him something. Did she owe him her attention? Why was he getting angry at her? Who was he? She turned to face him and he loomed over her like a bear, like nothing human. His anger had made him larger and stronger. He pulled and dragged her to the ground and ploughed her into the ground, tearing at her and mangling her. She fought with him because it would have been cowardly not to fight, even though she knew nothing could save her. She fought silently, disdaining to scream, and who would hear, what strangers would care? She arched her body sideways and fumbled for the knife in her boot. She found the knife and stabbed at him, not knowing where she wounded him. The wound angered him more, but did not slow him, and he wrenched the knife from her hand easily. He stabbed her accurately and with strength, just beneath the left breast, and the sharp pain interrupted the flow of the terrible, fantastic nightmare.

It ended. She gasped and was aware of voices, the people with the dog. She was aware of running footsteps and the clatter of the knife as it fell on the concrete pathway. She tried to call to the people with the dog, but she couldn't lift her voice high enough over the bushes around her. She imagined her voice as a ball she had to lift and throw over the bushes, but she couldn't do it, she was too weak. She heard the subway, far away and beneath her, the crowds running, all knowing where they were going, and the man in the crowd, running with them and frightened. She knew she would die and she wondered if they would catch the man, if he would be punished. She felt sorry for him, realizing the fear he must feel. She was much better off. She had nothing to worry about. She was relieved now, knowing she didn't have to worry about anything anymore. It was as if she had been running beside a moving train for such a long time, trying to get up enough speed and strength to jump on, and finally someone had reached out a strong arm and hauled her up and she was on her way. She'd caught her train. She raised her arm in the air but was too weak and let it drop; her hand fell to her breast and she felt the warm pool of her blood coming up through the wool shirt she wore. She smiled, she hummed, she was content. Already she could feel the vines growing up through her.

Epilogue

As a small child, Sia enjoyed lying on the floor of the kitchen and watching the muslin curtains blow softly inward on the breeze through the screen. She lived with her mother, Helen, in a four room, wood frame house in a neighborhood called Globeville, a little bit of country surrounded by the city of Denver, the highways, the stockyards and the smokestacks of factories.

The odors were horrendous and Helen burned incense stuck randomly in potted plants and simmered wild sage that she found in vacant lots in a saucepan on the range. Sia's father had given Helen the little house before he left, just in time to miss Sia's birth. Now Helen cleaned the houses of wealthy people and did some sewing.

One of the ladies had given Helen the baby grand piano that filled up their tiny living room, and she would play it all through the night until she fell asleep with her forehead on the music stand and her hands finally resting in her lap. She played magnificently, though it had been years since she had taken music lessons in her parents' house, a large mansion on Montview, a broad tree lined boulevard on the other side of the highway. Years later, after Helen had run away from home and gotten married and been disowned and had her daughter and been abandoned, after her parents died, she went back to the house she'd grown up in to clean it for the owners. She couldn't help sitting down at the old piano that had been left in the house, and she played it so wonderfully that the woman offered to give it to her. Helen tried to explain that it had been hers once, but the woman cut her off "yes, yes, I have heard about you" she said and ran off, apparently frightened, into another room. Nonetheless she had the piano delivered as she promised and she kept Helen on as help twice a week.

It was a dusky summer evening when the muslin curtains hit the range and caught fire while Helen played the Mozart Sonata in A and Sia slept on the kitchen floor. Sia felt the burning on her bare legs and finally woke, unbelieving and terrified as flames spread around her. The music continued in the front room and she ran to her mother, but her mother was lost in the music and didn't notice her daughter or the flames that followed Sia into the living room. Sia was screaming without making a sound and ran into the street where a neighbor picked her up and comforted her and told her the fire truck was on its way.

The music didn't stop until two firemen dragged her mother, protesting, away from the piano and out of the house. They couldn't save the house, but they saved her mother who fought with them. She was in such a frenzy that they took her to the hospital and Sia was sent to a shelter for abused and neglected children. When Sia asked if she could see her mother, a social worker told her she would see her soon, and that they were going to court. Sia didn't know what court was and the social worker wasn't sure how to explain it to a four year old.

When the Juvenile Court Magistrate found that a preponderance of the evidence showed it was not in Sia's best interest to be returned forthwith to her mother, Helen raised her powerful pianist's hands in supplication, not to the magistrate but directly to the gods who guided her. To the magistrate she issued one simple imperious command : "No, you must change your ruling! Don't you see I cannot live without my baby? I will die without my baby!"

Helen didn't die. In an effort to please the social worker and show her cooperation she committed herself voluntarily to Fort Logan Hospital for evaluation. She knew they would find her a perfect person. But the evaluating psychiatrist recommended a long term commitment and drug therapy.

Once a week, the social worker brought Sia to the hospital for a one hour supervised visit. Mother and daughter sat and stared at one another in a suffocating agony of restraint. Being watched, Sia would not go near her mother for a hug. Being overheard, Helen would not speak to Sia in the poetry that came naturally to her. The worker reported no apparent bonding between them and Sia was placed in the first of several group homes where they attempted to teach her to attach to other people. She was required to make a minimum number of appropriate peer contacts every day in order to earn points that accrued to buying privileges. Privileges could mean a movie, something special to eat or permission to stay alone in her room and read.

In her dreams she visited her mother and they plotted her escape. Several times Sia ran away and went to see her mother. She had to ride several buses or hitchhike if she couldn't panhandle bus fare and it took hours to get there. Then the Fort Logan staff would ask questions and trick her and send her back to social services. Eventually she was older and smarter and ran for herself.

She found some people, poets and musicians who shared an old Victorian house on 13th and Josephine Street and she stayed there. Her room was an attic dormer accessible by a winding and rickety outdoor staircase. It made her dizzy, the height and the freedom. One day she saw her mother wandering on Colfax but Helen didn't see her. She was listening to the voices. Sia took her arm and guided her back to her house, slowly and with difficulty, up the stairs. Her mother was heavier now and the stairs creaked and sagged. But Helen followed docilely and she lay down as she was told on Sia's bed in her little room.

She did not respond when Sia told her she would be right back with groceries, but when Sia returned, not more than forty minutes later, her mother was gone. She ran up and down the street calling Helen's name, but Helen didn't answer and was nowhere to be seen. Sia cried hard all through the night and her eyes were swollen and sore for days. That was the last time she saw her mother, the last time she cried for her mother. She was sixteen. Jack Kerouac was her idol. She hitchhiked to San Francisco. She began creating her life as a work of art and dedicated it to Helen.

The Nun: A Short Story

Short Story Version of The Nun: Preface

The first edition of *The Nun*, was published in 1992. While not a runaway bestseller, it did elicit enthusiastic appreciation from a handful of readers who offered a variety of interpretations as to its meaning. The general consensus seemed to be that the book was about art and death.

The internet has rejuvenated and broadened the connections between many authors and readers, myself included, and the first edition of *The Nun* was reviewed some years ago in an online journal titled The Ultimate Hallucination, by J. R. Parker who asked in an introductory paragraph: "What deeper thought drives the creative mind? Exactly where does inspiration come from and how is the artist able to channel it into a medium comprehensible to the masses?"

While I would hardly characterize my readership as "the masses" I am as fascinated by this question as Mr. Parker and flattered that he assumed I had set forth intentionally to answer this question when I wrote *The Nun*. He even states that I had hopes of enlightening readers on this point. However I must admit that I had no such intentions or hopes when I began writing and the inspiration for this story was a wonderful mystery to me.

The Nun was my first novel begun nearly fifteen years before its first publication. Part I was inspired. I don't use the term euphemistically but literally. Walks in the forest and listening to tapes of medieval music were intended to be relaxing pleasures but the result was a vision. I transcribed the story as it came to me and I remember the voice in my mind as if it came from outside. It was finished in two weeks and I never rewrote a single word (although I did *add* a few words about stone sculpting after researching that art). Part II, which Mr. Parker in his review and indeed every reader who took time to write to me about the book, noticed was radically different from Part I, was a willed, intentionally crafted piece of writing. I intentionally created a voice more modern than the voice that came from some misty past but there was also an unintentional difference which I must admit came from the fact that the source of inspiration for Part I was simply not there. Part I had a transcendent quality that I simply could not intentionally reproduce (putting me in my place).

It could be said that the two parts set in different centuries with different, albeit *related*, voices, comprise a virtual demonstration of the difference between pure inspiration and disciplined, directed, *intended* creative writing. Looking back with over twenty years of objectivity I'd say that is yet another layer I've discovered in this work, which brings me around to my latest theory on the matter of the muse. I have come to believe that art is a means by which the artist expands insight into the self as part of the larger world. Just as human beings could not see microorganisms until someone "invented" the microscope (was this a "discovery" or an "inspiration" and what is the difference? I wonder), literature, beginning with the most ancient tales, has been the lens whereby human beings may examine their own otherwise unseen motives. In both cases, interpretations of what is seen vary with the observer.

The short story version that follows exists because as a returning college student in my thirties I found myself required to write a short story in order to gain admittance to an advanced fiction workshop with J.R. Salamanca (a wonderful writer and teacher). I had long ago discarded the slick and trivial short fictions of my youth and had only novellas to submit. I decided to cut down the first part of *The Nun* to short story length and in so doing actually changed its direction (and perhaps its meaning). Jack, by the way, pronounced the story "perfect" and that praise coming from a writer of his caliber was exhilarating.

Sandra Shwayder Sanchez
FKA Sandra Shwayder
Spring 2010

The Nun: A Short Story

I.

Each woman had, in addition to the communal tasks of chanting and prayer, a practical task to accomplish. One supervised the young girls who came from outside to work in the weaving room. In exchange for their labor they learned a trade and learned it well. Another of the nuns oversaw other girls in the laundry work or the kitchen. All the nuns helped in the garden. Their sustenance depended on it and they could get no one else to come to help with this vital work. Odyssia was one who spent more time in the garden, daily in fact, whatever the weather and all day during certain seasons. She had no other task. All spring and summer she worked her long hard day, but in the fall when the harvest had been dried, hung, pickled and stored, Sia found herself with entire afternoons free to spend in the woods. During one of her walks in the woods when the forest seemed woven of contrasting and mellowing greens and reds, she met Magi.

Sia was curious when she first met Magi whether she was a man or a woman: she never really could be sure. But she preferred to think that Magi was female and Magi herself didn't seem to care. She was very square, too solid to be considered fat, with the beginnings of breasts and very strong mannish arms and hands. She had a mustache and was most extraordinarily hairy all over her body and face. Her facial features were badly molded, thick and rouged in and her skin was bumpy and pitted. She dressed in filthy men's clothing and large boots.

The first time Sia saw her in the woods she was frightened and hid in a ravine formed by a dried stream. As she watched from her hiding place in the leaves, she saw Magi choose a newly felled log. She stripped off the bark and caressed the wood, touching and examining it and this intrigued Sia. Later Sia followed Magi through the woods to a small hut built of logs filled in with mud and roofed with long grasses dried in the sun. Nearby was another log hut, three-sided with a roof and filled with beautifully carved wooden figures. The figures were all that Magi was not: tall and thin with flowing drapery revealing only slightly the full feminine shapes of hips and breasts beneath. The faces were thin with long sharp noses and large eyes under exquisitely sculpted lids. Oddly enough, the lips were not well done. But the hands were the best of all: long, thin-fingered hands delicately holding goblets or flowers or the folds of a robe.

Every day that fall, Sia followed Magi through the woods and when Magi was away from the hut she went herself to get a closer look at the statues. She examined them carefully as she listened for Magi's approach and she was also careful to note the light in order to know the time and be back in time for the evening meal and prayers. Often she wondered if she shouldn't wait for Magi and speak to her and ask if she could learn to carve figures herself. She always ended up deciding against it because Magi's appearance frightened her.

But it was meant that she learn this art and one afternoon in late November Magi surprised Sia among the statues. Sia stood quietly waiting for Magi's reaction and carefully concealed her own fear. Magi was kind from the start and Sia never told her of her fear, not wishing to offend her.

Magi talked hardly at all, the shortest possible conversation made her hoarse and over-excited. She had lived alone in the woods for many years with only the trees for company. When she realized that Sia wanted to learn the art of carving she agreed to teach her with a brusque nod of her head. She used gestures and only the few words absolutely necessary to instruct Sia in the selection and preparation of the wood. Sia spent her afternoons carving the blocks of wood Magi allotted to her. Magi guided her silently and Sia worked slowly and patiently, feeling she had forever to learn and confident that she would learn all she needed to create the most perfect statues in wood and later, she hoped, in stone.

She learned to look for trees that had died from drought or had frozen in an unusually harsh winter, trees that died perfect, not maimed by disease or rot, their limbs still reaching and graceful, the bark slowly dropping off as the dead wood inside dried and shrank inward. Such wood could be used almost as soon as they found it. But still they cut living trees. The forest was generous. And these, dripping with sap, their translucent, succulent tree blood, were set upright in the drying shed where they might stand for years before they could be carved. These trees had been alive, still showed signs of life, took years to completely lose their livingness and Sia felt a rapport with them. Walking in the woods she imagined herself floating among the bones of her own body. And she realized she knew the trees more intimately than she knew Magi or the other nuns in the convent. She too had stopped talking and resented it when the nuns made small talk around her and interrupted her ponderings, as if their chatter somehow cut her off from her introspective destination. She felt that she understood Magi and between them speech was not necessary and that among those who did not understand her, speech was not useful. The singing, the abstract flowing of human sound soothed her and made vivid the visions she sought. She grew to love the singing, to crave it, and she kept it always in her mind as a kind of guide to the inner-most whorls of her own history, her soul's as yet unlived memories. And even this modulated sound of the living present she could only tolerate at a distance very far and faint or very close, vibrating in her head: either extreme of distance acoustically distorted and dehumanized the music, moving it from exterior reality to interior vision. And thus everything she touched, heard, smelled, saw, she internalized, absorbed into her dream, made ancient and distant, all her senses working to illuminate that memory lost in such a deep dark place in her soul.

If anyone noticed her growing introspection, they would naturally attribute it to a strong religious vocation and no one tried seriously to intrude upon her waking dream. Moving as she did through myriad simultaneous incarnations, the ordinary time of the convent passed unnoticed: winter, spring, summer, fall: she couldn't quite tell how many of them, and often she simply telescoped all the summers into one, all the winters into one. It might have been two years that passed as she carved, instead of ten. But then she'd take a log that she had cut fresh and living from the forest and it was ready now for her tools and then she'd know that she was growing older.

II.

I am still the green and golden child
Visioning elves and warriors in the whorled bark
I am again the oaken crone brittle
The wind is my terror and my secret joy
My hand, like a gourd,
Holds pain and poisoned scents
My hand, like a gourd, collects
Rains of wine and vinegar

Sia hungered for the wood and felt nourished by it even while, in fact, she was growing thinner with actual hunger. The fall harvest had not been good and late frosts the spring before had blighted the blossoms on the fruit trees so that now there were no fruits to dry and store against the long winter. With careful organization, the abbess always got them through the winters, lean or plentiful, the stores of food each year were rationed accordingly. This year no one ever felt fully satisfied but no one starved. It was not so among the neighboring country men and women. Although everyone started out with the same experience, the same understanding of the facts of their existence, dependent on the weather and the whims of the Gods (oh, yes they worshipped "God" but always there was the undercurrent of paganism, of wheedling and appeasing and raillery against the myriad gods of unpredictable chance, of frosts or hail, drought or molding damp, of insects and animals and even human forgetfulness and laziness and exhaustion and despair), although everyone started the season with the same understanding of what lay ahead, they all used this knowledge differently. Knowing this, the abbess did not judge as stupid or lazy or extravagant the repeated poor planning of her neighbors. Nor did she know they judged her arrogant. But in accepting as normal their extremes, reaping extravagant joy one day (a joy measured in wine and food) and giving violent expression to their suffering and poverty the next, she saw no need or perhaps no hope in trying to change them, to organize their minds and lives, to even out the chasms between want and plenty, to help them. She accepted them, ignored them and let nature take its course.

Meantime the nuns in their convent, like well-organized ants, weathered the seasons with little variation from year to year, mostly unaware of the ups and downs of their neighbors. As Sia became more and more aloof from the convent community itself, she was even less aware of the outside world, not even listening to the bits of gossip that rippled through the kitchen and workrooms. The relationship of the nuns to the world around them was largely a matter of rumor and innuendo, never really clear to anyone, but each woman had her own perception subtly different from all the others, and responded with her own personal reaction of fear or contempt or relief. Sia alone had ceased entirely to think about it, the outside world. She was totally surrounded by images of perfect beauty unmarred by the incongruities of human personality. She felt herself grained and old and immune as oak.

All around them resentment festered poisoning the air, perversely nourished by the famine and the deaths of children. The nuns, sensing it, could not gauge it. Sia was completely unaware of it. In the evenings, walking back to prayers, Sia measured the distance yet to go by the chants of the nuns, their voices drifting like mist through the trees to her and only becoming real when she entered the chambers of stone. She was so accustomed to this sound she often heard it at other times and places, deeper in the woods where she couldn't possibly hear them, and yet she did hear them, her memory twisting the random sounds of crickets and birds and streams into the orderly plain song of nuns singing through stone. This evening the singing sound reached her earlier and she thought nothing of it, but as she came closer, within sight of the convent, she became aware uneasily of the discordances and abruptness and then she heard quite clearly the screams. Sia stopped to listen carefully and let this confusion of sound and hallucination straighten itself out and then, yes, it was screaming, the screaming of women in terror and pain and mingled with this the almost good-humored yells of men, and laughing: men laughing and women screaming ... and dying. Screams forced out of them with the air squeezed out of their lungs and the blood spurting out of their innards around the thick bodies of the men. The men were extravagant, reaping their harvest of despair. They had taken the food stored up by the nuns and now were taking the women, raping and killing them and laughing because now there would also be death in the convent as well as their huts. They were all equal, grieving and screaming before God. No one understood it. It had taken a long time and the vengeful energy of two or three men with dead or dying children, starving children. Already some of the men were worried that they would be punished for their sin. But others had learned that all is chance and their God was indifferent, malicious and life was his joke. They hadn't reasoned it out in their minds: they knew it in their brutal souls. But regardless of God, regardless of sin and punishment or the vicissitudes of pure chance, there it was, a courtyard full of the dozen dead and dying women. Anyone who still whimpered was quickly put out of her misery and the women were pyred in the courtyard atop their own heavy furnishings and tapestries. After the convulsions of slaughter came the calm of necessity. This one time the countrymen were well organized. While some stayed to cremate the bodies, others packed up their booty of dried peas and flour, oil and wine and carefully conveyed them to their families, distributing everything equally among their numbers and rationing it all out to last the winter.

It had been a small convent and an early forerunner of a mass movement, remote and isolated, and a world plagued with wars and heresies and more far reaching resentments paid no attention to its end.

Sia herself was initially unaffected by what happened. Like a terrible nightmare it had traumatized her while she watched, but once over, its implications gave way to more mundane anxieties. For two or three days she was totally concerned with fear for herself and hid in the woods, hungry, damp and freezing but hardly daring to move. She listened to the crackle of the burning timbers and the crash of unsupported stones, trying to detect behind these noises the sounds of men. But the men were gone. Then she began to move cautiously back through the woods to Magi's hut. It was an agonizing slow walk, straining for silence, stopping to listen, mistrustful of the silence and afraid of every sound. It took an entire day to get to Magi's and then she found Magi dead also.

Magi must have been dead for as long as Sia had been gone and was beginning to smell slightly despite the cold. When Sia saw her teacher dead she approached a desperate longing to find that it was another vision, a mistake and when she realized it was not a dream, that there was no mistake, Sia broke three, four days (she didn't know) of silence and screamed, a scream of terror, thinking Magi was another victim of the peasants. But why? She had nothing they could want or envy. Superstition perhaps? Had they thought she was a witch bringing misfortunes? It could happen Sia knew. But Magi's body, when Sia looked more calmly, not for signs of life this time but for signs of the cause of death, was not mutilated and her expression was not stricken or afraid.

Sia thought what had to be done. Magi's body had to be buried. Lacking strength to carry it, she used patience and ingenuity to lever and roll the heavy body into a shallow ravine. First she covered the body with leaves, the matted damp leaves of the forest floor, and with thick pieces of moss that she peeled off rocks in the stream with bark she peeled from trees. There was nowhere she could dig soil for this grave, the ground was woven through with roots holding down the thinnest layer of soil over rock. She took rushes meant for roofing and then she began to gather stones. She was all night carrying stones to the grave. Her eyes became accustomed to the dark and she thought constantly of vultures and wild dogs and carried the stones until morning when she could see it was enough.

After her long night of labor, after the many nights of exhausting terror, Sia now slept in Magi's hut from shortly after sunrise to shortly after sunrise the next day. All during this sleep, she kept dreaming of waking and seeing people, the men, the murderers, talking rationally to her as if nothing had happened and herself trying to talk back to them, but unable to, feeling too tired, feeling pulled down by the heavy tiredness in her body and for a long time after she really did wake up she thought they had been there.

It was hours before she realized she had been asleep and dreaming a day and night, maybe several days and nights: she could not be sure. She had to go back to the grave she had made to realize that indeed Magi was dead and indeed she had witnessed the rape and murder of all the nuns. There was no one left.

III.

Magi had made and set traps for small animals which she cooked with wild herbs she found growing in the woods. Sia walked where she had seen Magi walk to check the traps. Two were empty but in the third an animal had bled to death. The stench and the buzzing of flies disgusted her and she did not go near it. She examined the other traps to see how they were set, sprang one and reset it and left them. She would check them twice daily as she knew Magi had done and kill whatever animals she found struggling in them with a blow to the head. Magi had been quick and sure and the animals had died quickly, stunned painlessly into death. Sia's first attempts were clumsy and, overcome with guilt and panic, she smashed and maimed squealing rabbits and squirrels which were then not fit to eat and she dreamed their slow agonized and bewildered sufferings nightly. To her the worst thing was that those little animals didn't understand why she doing this to them. With practice she may have become more adept but the business revolted her and she hung the traps up loose in Magi's hut.

The stream ran too fast for the winter frost to catch and hold it and the water was constantly warmed by new water gushing out of the warm innards of the earth. Fish thrived in it and so did cress and mint and bitter greens she didn't know. There was no grain for her or milk or eggs and she was often sick while her body worked to adjust to the constant unchanging diet of fish and bitter greens. Nausea and diarrhea wracked her body violently for hours and she was left exhausted and longing for a bowl of warm milk. She learned to fast every three days and drink large quantities of the good water fresh from the spring.

Sia used herbs the way she had seen Magi use them. She boiled some to drink or to season her food, some she used as cures for cuts or rashes. There was one plant hanging in the hut that she couldn't find in the woods and she had seen Magi partake of it only once, after she had left for a day and merely looked back for some reason now forgotten. What she remembered was the look on Magi's face as she prepared the herb in boiling water to drink, as if preparing for a ritual. Now Sia tried it. Her stomach reacted ominously and she laid herself down in the stream. She lay there for along time while the soothing water calmed her pains and cooled her fever. She thought she may have fallen asleep and dreamed because she began to perceive the world differently. Things that shouldn't move came closer to her and closer as she watched them growing in magnitude and she felt herself disintegrating into them, into leaves or bark or water. Light and dark took on mass so that shadows seemed as real, more real than the objects casting them. The divisions between objects became lost or changed and her gaze transformed the universe into an unfamiliar system of geometrics. Leaves were suspended from above by solid shafts of light and the trees grew horizontally along the ground in the paths of their shadows. She got up and was afraid to walk into shadow, feeling the tactile hallucinations of collision. The shadows were as walls to her and she stayed in the stream, not knowing where she could safely walk. Breezes she could not feel caused the smallest leaves and wild flowers to tremble and then she could not remember if she had seen their trembling or felt it and it seemed important to her to remember. She began to cry and then she slept. She could tell the difference between her visions and her dreams because her dreams were completely fantastic and impossible whereas her visions had been merely confusing. In her dreams the leaves and trees disappeared and returned, different ones in different places. And there were no longer reds and golds and greens of early autumn but fantastic colors she had only seen in books at the convent, colors she had no names for. And she flew or rather swam through the air running away from someone who called her name and seemed alternately friendly and vicious and sometimes they both turned into stone and struggled to move through the stone or carry it with them and all the feelings she felt she knew for certain her pursuer felt also to the same degree and at the same time. But she knew she was not her own pursuer. And then in her dream she fell asleep, into a deeper sleep, dreamless except for the knowledge that she didn't dream, except for the knowledge of darkness and quiet and rest.

Sia awoke free of hallucinations but she could feel things before she touched them and enjoyed greater clarity of vision. She felt enormously rested. After ignoring God for many years, she now praised God for sending her strength. She began to mumble to herself the prayers that had lost their meaning in the convent and yet had been the secret accompaniment to her life. All her waking moments she mumbled and chanted, keeping her voice to a whisper, not daring to intrude her voice on the forest's silence, not daring to stop her litany of praise, of apology. She did not try to fathom the sense of it. She did not know that she was lonely. God became her friend and her prayers, formal and musical, gave way to conversations, incessant and desperate chatter. She now felt a trio of personalities, herself old and solitary, the young nun she was and another observer, a spectator of their conversations and activity. She slept more and sat thinking, dreaming or watching her dreams dream themselves and she carved less and less. She reproached herself for not working, she had always worked hard at something. She tried the last remains of the mysterious herb. It was winter now. Snow fell and silenced the world. Sia fell silent too, listening to the conversations of the old hermit and the young nun, to the voices, no longer making sense of the words. Together they went through the ritual of drinking the herb tea. Together they went through the ritual of crushing it and brewing it and drinking it facing each other over the fire and they multiplied around the fire until a crowd of women went out together into the forest, leaving their tracks through the newly fallen snow. Sia felt them fanning out from her sides like angels in pictures and heard their singing faint as though from a great distance although she knew they were right beside her and in her and they moved as one.

IV.

In the spring the stream flooded, growing wild and turbulent and wrecked the homesteads built too close to its banks. In the havoc, animals ran into the forest and were lost and in this way Sia acquired some chickens and a young cow about to calf. The chickens roosted in trees and Sia searched the woods each morning for eggs, sparse at first, becoming more frequent as the weather warmed. The cow made do with meadow grasses less than an hour's walk away. There was clover there and a variety of wild flowers. She became attached to the cow with her great liquid brown eyes. In the absence of human sounds, the cackling of the chickens and the cow's occasional mooing became like speech. She seemed to understand it as such. The cow particularly seemed to develop personality. After Sia guided her to the meadow to graze and back to the stream to drink and then to the shelter of the forest around Magi's hut, she began to go through the routine herself and to forge her own path through the woods. She was young, Sia could tell. Her udder was so small it was barely visible under her bulging belly. She was, in fact, still a heifer and the calf would be her first. When the time came she was completely quiet and bewildered and even frightened and Sia could tell something was wrong. Something about the way the head and one foot just stayed there while the mother heaved and pushed and struggled with this bewildering discomfort. Sia remembered watching a man, an uncle, when she was a child, pushing the head of a calf back inside the mother and reaching up inside the mother up to his shoulder to grab the front legs and pull them out. Sia was long and thin and the years spent working with wood had made her strong. She pushed hard against the mother to get the head back inside. But she couldn't find the other hoof. Somehow one of the legs was tangled inside the mother and Sia couldn't find it. She pulled out of the cow and stood a moment to rest. The exhausted animal fell to her side, giving up and Sia tried to coax her up to her feet again. She began to yell and to kick, kicking the animal mercilessly in her panic to save the cow and calf. The cow got to her feet and walked a few steps away, keeping her back away from Sia. She tried to rub the emerging head off against a tree, backing over and over into the tree and then trying to run and she fell again, and again Sia kicked her to her feet and pushed the head back, resisting the inexorable, disastrous birth. The third time the head came out flanked by both legs, the hooves pointed skyward. The head was wrapped in a grey membrane, long lashed eyes closed as if dead, at any rate not yet alive, utterly still. The heifer was tired, not pushing so hard now. The head and hooves stayed there, a dead weight. Sia tied a rope she had hanging with the traps in Magi's hut around the hooves and then wound it once around a tree and she began to pull. Inch by inch she pulled the calf out of the mother. She could feel the tearing inside the mother as she pulled until she was nearly lying on the ground, held up only by the tension of the rope. And then the calf was out. It lay on the ground beside the exhausted and peaceful mother, covered with blood and the grey membrane, the eyes still closed tight and still. Sia reached out a hand to touch it gently, fearing it was dead. With surprising energy the little animal butted her when she touched him and joyously she ran for water to wash him. When she returned the mother was placidly licking the calf, contented and wise and thoughtless.

V.

When the calf was old enough, Sia arranged her statues, took a last look at them and the hut and the forest and set out on the road with the cow by her side and the calf trotting behind. She had washed Magi's old trousers and cloak although they would always retain the color and odor of smoke and exchanged her female clothing for these. She walked barefoot and cut off all her hair. Starvation and exposure and hard work had aged and neutered her and other travelers knew not whether she was male or female and assumed she must be a man, traveling alone like that with the animals. She looked for farm work and lived in hay-lots with her cows and she never spoke except to her animals. She passed for a mute and a man for the remainder of her long life and watched the rituals of family and society from a close proximity, although she was an exile in time, living as lightly and invisibly as a ghost on the surface of the years. But she was ever happy, never forgetting that God had allowed her the life of the mother and child. When she died, her secret was exposed and she left a legacy of mystery and speculation. Meantime, in the woods, the statues were discovered and because they bore a strong resemblance to the nuns murdered long ago, the local country men and women were in awe of them and set them up in the ruined courtyard of the convent, laying offerings of grain and wine at their feet in supplication for a bountiful harvest.

About the Author

Sandra Shwayder Sanchez earned a BA in Behaviorial Sciences at University of Md. and a Juris Doctor degree from Denver University Law School. Her law practice involved the representation of indigent clients in the Denver criminal, family and mental health courts as well as civil rights work with Penfield Tate II before his death in 1993. In the early seventies she built a house and farmed in rural West Virginia. She now lives in a small mountain town in Colorado with her husband Ed Sanchez

Novels by Sandra Shwayder Sanchez:
  Stillbird
  The Secret of A Long Journey

Collections by Sandra Shwayder Sanchez:
  Three Novellas
  A Mile in These Shoes